BLACK DIAMONDS,

YELLOW APPLES

AN "EY UP, MI DUCK!" PUBLICATION

Black Diamonds, Yellow Apples

A working-class Derbyshire childhood between the wars

by

ELSIE GADSBY

With illustrations by the author

SCOLLINS & TITFORD

49 St. Mary Street, Ilkeston, Derbys.

I SBN 0 9505292 5 7

Published by: Scollins & Titford, 49 St. Mary Street, Ilkeston, Derbyshire.
Printed by. Wm. J. Butler & Co., Station Road, Bulwell, Nottingham.

CONTENTS

THE FAMILY

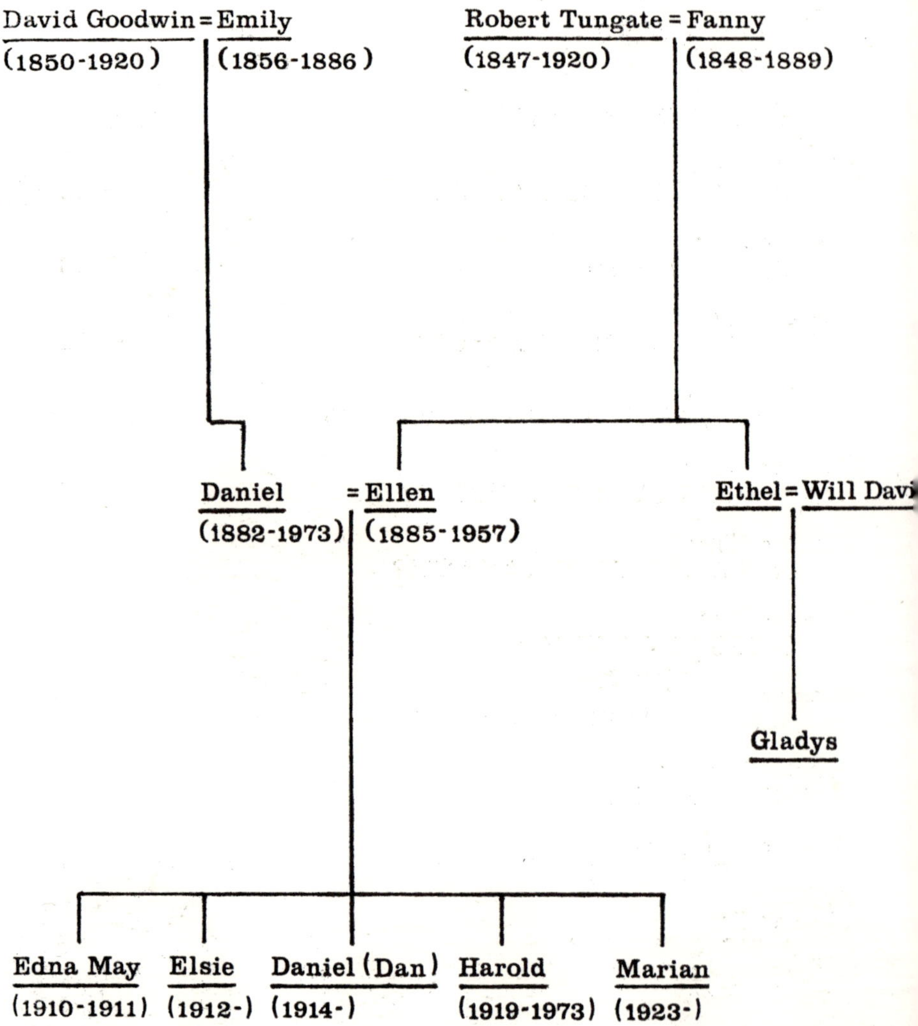
David Goodwin = Emily
(1850-1920) (1856-1886)
Robert Tungate = Fanny
(1847-1920) (1848-1889)
Daniel = Ellen
(1882-1973) (1885-1957)
Ethel = Will Davi
Gladys
Edna May
(1910-1911)
Elsie
(1912-)
Daniel (Dan)
(1914-)
Harold
(1919-1973)
Marian
(1923-)

THE GOODWIN FAMILY

Daniel

Ellen

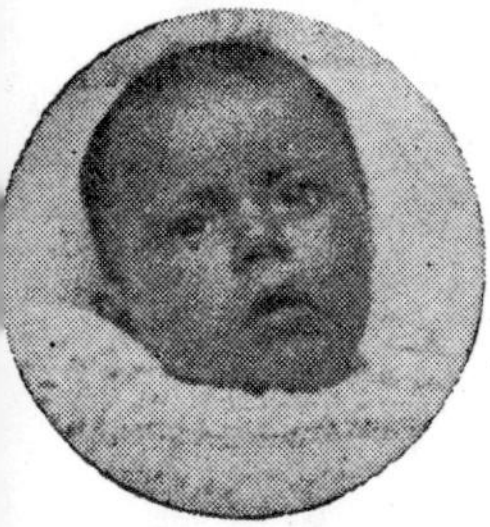
Edna May

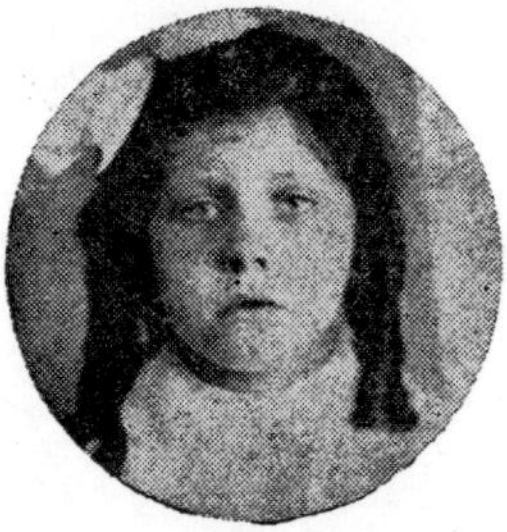
Elsie

Dan

Harold

Marian

THE DAVIS FAMILY

Will

Ethel

Gladys

SHIPLEY WOODSIDE COLLIERY
where Dan Goodwin worked
Derbys.
TRAM TERMINUS
Notts.
COTMANHAY
'YELLOW APPLES'
Cotmanhay Road
TH'OLLER
FACTORY
River Erewash
Erewash Canal
Derbyshire
NOTTINGHAM
Ilkeston
DERBY
Bath Steet
Ilkeston
CEMETERY
CINEMA
MARKET PLACE

To Aunt Ethel and Uncle Will

for all the happiness they gave me.

Chapter One

IN the beginning there was Dan. He was my brother — a thin, dark-haired, pale little thing. He was a bit younger than me, by about a year and a half. There'd been another girl before me, Edna May. But she'd died of a wasting disease when she was almost two.

And then, of course, there was Mam and Dad. Mam was big and bonny. I suppose she would be classed as overweight now. Every so often she would be bigger than ever — or rather her tummy would be. Then there'd be another brother or sister.

She'd got arms like a navvy and a vocabulary to match. One smack from her, and you did as you were told.

Dad, now, was quiet. A rather gaunt man, with a big long nose ("aristocratic" he used to call it), the warmest brown eyes, and a gentle manner He was a collier, 'daytler', a man who cleared the muck away after a fall. He was the lowest-paid worker in the pit.

But above all he was a dreamer, an idealist. "Someday," he would say, his head in the clouds, "someday we'll have a cottage of our own, an' a nice big garden — you'll see."

"Aye? And when'll that be?" our mam would ask.

"When me ship comes in. Just wait and see."

"Tha bloody ship'll sink before that day comes," she'd taunt him. " 'Sides — where d'yer think the money'll come from?"

"Other folks have rich relatives die and leave them summat," he'd answer hopefully.

He was always scanning the Lost Property and Unclaimed Money column in the Sunday papers. But there was never a Goodwin on the list. I think Goodwins must have been the poorest people in Britain.

"Then when me ship does come in I'll buy thee a sewing machine," he'd tell me.

How I dreamed of that sewing machine. It would be a treadle. Lovely shiny brown wood, and the iron frame underneath all glossy black, and outlined with gold.

My Aunty at Nottingham had one. She used to sew pointed net caps for fitting over horses' ears during the Summer months. She'd treadle away like mad, rattling and banging, slipping the net pieces under the foot automatically, and only stopping to fill a shuttle or make herself a cup of tea.

Oh — how I'd polish that machine when I got it. Then I'd be able to make myself flannelette nighties, and Mam's winceyette petticoats, and those funny camisoles she wore. Closet seats, she called them; just a long rectangle with a hole in the middle to put her head through, and tapes at each corner to tie around her waist.

Flannelette nighties were another of my dreams. Up till about the age of nine or ten, I wore Dad's old union shirts. When the neck band had frayed too much and the shirt lap had worn too thin, Mam would cut them level, lopping off three or four inches, then she'd give them to me to sew. But they were warm. I could wrap my knees up in the voluminous garment.

But the sewing machine never materialised, and Dad's ship never came in. And I sewed and sewed until my fingers grew sore, and Mam would say:

"Put it down for a bit, there's allus another day. Besides you'll strain your eyes, and I can't afford no specs."

I always seemed to be sewing. I can't remember when I first started. I must have been born with a needle in my fingers, same as they say some kids had a silver spoon in their mouths. Or else a pencil in my fingers. I was always drawing. If I could get hold of a bit of paper, some wallpaper, or even a blank column on the edge of a newspaper and a stub of pencil, I was happy enough. It just came naturally, I suppose, same as same people can sing or act, or play the piano.

And read! Heavens — if I got hold of a book I'd never hear a word off Mam until she'd uptip my chair with a toe end.

"Mam — don't do that," I'd say, "I just got to a good part."

"I'll 'good part' you if you don't answer me when I talk to you — get these pots washed," she'd say. Well, there was no arguing with that voice of authority, but I'd look rebellious until Dad interposed:

"Better do as yer Mam says. Then yer can read afterwards."

And he'd wink at me.

But Mam wasn't so bad really, I suppose. I expect having to skimp and scrape so much made her short-tempered at times. Many a time she'd say, "Leave that. You just finish this bit of sewing," and she'd praise me when the garment was finished.

But always I'd dream of that sewing machine.

Dan, now, was always going on about a bike. We knew he'd never get one. Well — there was just never any money to spare. But it doesn't cost any money to dream, does it?

He was always thin as a rake, no matter how many suet dumplings Mam pushed into him. We were inseparable. We went everywhere together; apart from being in class, that is. But we went to school together, and were together after tea. Of course when we played we had to put on old clothes.

We had a "den" built on "th'oller", a piece of waste ground at the bottom of our street.

We would gather bits of wood, and a few cobbles of coal nicked from the coalhouse. Our pockets bulging with little spuds and onions which we'd secretly purloined from the pantry, we would make for th'oller.

Our friends woud be there, mostly boys. I think I must have looked like a boy — I was accepted as one. Then we would start our fire, first making a square with bricks. When we'd got the wood and coal burning well we put our bit of tin across. I never did find out whose dustbin lid that tin came off. . .

We would sit round the smoky fire and tell our stories. We made them up, of course; often thought up weird tortures we'd inflict on our teachers.

Then with a pop the potatoes would be ready, the onions sizzling and smelling delicious, and we'd burn our fingers trying to get the skins off. There was never anything which tasted quite as delightful as those soil-caked potatoes and onions, nor has there ever been since.

By the time we'd been sitting by our fire for a couple of hours we looked like the Kentucky Minstrels. Black faces where the smoke had blown on us, and white around our eyes and where we'd licked around our mouths. Then, when it had begun to get dark, we'd hear our mothers calling us.

"Albe-r-r-t — Mai-i-sy. Come on. Bedtime."

Then our Mam:

"Elsi-e-e — Dan-e e-e," and reluctantly we'd say our good-byes.

"See you tomorrow, Bert, 'night Perce, 'night Maisie."

But when we got in the warmth of the house, gosh — you should have smelled our clothes.

"Good God — what a stink!" Mam would say. "Off with 'em. An' you can get across to that wash'ouse an' get that muck off yer faces. An' tomorrow yer'll stop in. Coming home like that — I'll show yer!"

But by the next night she'd forgotten all about it. I don't think she really minded, so long as we put our old clothes on.

Dad never used to interfere. Besides, he was usually on the afternoon shift, and didn't get home until well after ten at night. Mam would have the boiler beside the old iron fireplace full, and a arge pancheon waiting on the pegged rug, with a coarse linen towel hanging ready on the fire-guard. And on the few times I was allowed to stay up I was always amazed to see that he washed just down to the waist. There was still a dark grey line showing at the top of his trousers, and although he rubbed away at his face, there was still a smudge of coal dust around his eyes, almost as if he'd got mascara on, and it had got wet and run.

There were no pit baths then. All that came much later, as did the pit-top canteens.

And then once a week, the long tin bath would be lifted off the outside washhouse wall and put in front of the fire. The boiler would be kept full, with the kettle steaming on the hob, and a large iron saucepan boiling away.

Then would start the weekly bath ritual. Kids first, all in the same water. Then the bath would be emptied, a bucket full at a time, while we ate our bread and dripping and drank our cocoa.

Then Mam would start pouring hot water again, and fetching cold water from across the yard. Then they'd start on their baths. Only by this time we kids were all in bed, talking and giggling. After a few minutes Mam would shout upstairs:

"If yer don't shut up I'll come an' smack yer arses!"

That would quieten us, and we'd soon be off to sleep. And my dreams would be a jumbled medley of sewing machines, frilly flannelette nighties, smoky potatoes and onions, pencils and paints. And in the background there'd always be Mam and Dad waiting to bring sanity back into my life next morning.

Chapter Two

I WAS only two years old when the first war started — The Great War — and six when peace was declared; so I don't remember much about it. The earliest thing I do remember was when I had diphtheria. Children used to die of the disease then. There were no innoculations such as children have now, only isolation. I suppose I was one of the lucky ones.

I must have been about three at the time. I can distinctly remember being lifted up in the arms of a nurse or sister and waving my podgy arms at Mam and Dad outside. That's all. Just the memory of them framed in the window, like a picture.

The next few years are almost a blank in my mind. Apart from references to The Kaiser and the Bloody Hun, the only other thing I recollect about that war was when my Uncle Will came to see us. He was in the Cavalry, and right handsome he looked in his leather leggings and his khaki trousers which bulged out around his thighs. He wore a peaked khaki hat, too, and had the loveliest pair of moustaches. To me he was a hero.

It was Christmas when he came on leave, and he and Aunt Ethel (the one who had the sewing machine) came to stay, bringing their little girl, my cousin Gladys. She'd be four or five at the time.

Then, unexpectedly, along came another Aunt. Aunt Lizzie was Mam's eldest sister, and a real beauty, with the loveliest deep-set brown eyes I've ever seen. Her husband, Uncle Arthur, looked the spitting image of King George the Fifth, who was on the throne then. He had pointed moustaches and a brown beard pointed at the bottom. Oh, they were a right handsome pair.

They all stayed the night, but where they slept heaven alone knows. We only had two bedrooms, so some of them must have slept in the parlour.

The hilarious part about this Christmas visit was that everybody insisted on hanging up a stocking, not just the youngsters.

Of course we kids (there were five of us with the cousins) got the usual small toys, apples and oranges and toffee in our bulging black woollen stockings next morning.

But we were in a fever of impatience to see what Mam and Dad and the Aunts and Uncles had got. Just imagine what the fireplace must have looked like. Five kids' stockings in a row on the fireguard, and the six adults' socks and stockings hanging from the mantlepiece or chairbacks.

And when they started to empty them, oh my, the hilarity of it all! Besides cigarettes and tobacco, there were carrots, turnips, pieces of coal, anything that must have been available to the pre-

tend Santas. And then, right at the bottom of the men's socks were mysterious-looking wet parcels which smelt to high heaven. And inside was horse manure, now moist and pungent from the warmth of the overnight fire. What a Christmas.

Shortly after that Mam had another baby. There was never any fuss. One day there'd be nappies fetched out and washed. Mam would change both beds, take down all the curtains and have a right good clean up of the whole house.

Then a few nights later there'd be a fire in the front bedroom, with a clothes horse full of baby things warming in front. I know, because one night my curiosity got the better of me, and I crept into the front bedroom to see what mysterious happenings were going on. I must have stood for a long time, just gaping, as realization dawned on me.

Mam must have heard me, for she lumbered slowly up the stairs.

"What yer doin' in there, nosy bogger? Go on, get to bed."

Well I went to bed, but I couldn't sleep. I could hear voices, and Dad was calling up to Mam: "Here's Mrs Sisson."

Mrs Sisson, I learned later, was the midwife. She was round, wore a navy felt hat and cape, had whiskers sprouting from her chin, and she waddled. And she liked her beer. I'd heard it said often that she always expected a jug of beer to be ready when she called on a maternity case, but I don't know how much of this was just hearsay.

Well for hours that night I just lay listening. I can remember hearing grunts and groans, and commands to "push now — push." I must have have fallen sleep then, for when I woke it was morning. Mam was calling to me, gently. And slowly I crept into her room, not knowing what I might find. And there was Mam, sitting up drinking a cup of tea, and with a new baby brother in her bed.

I think that was when I first began to feel the pangs of jealousy.

One day, whilst Mam was still in bed, she fancied an egg for her tea. Now teatime at our house was strictly a bread and jam, bread and dripping affair. An egg for tea! It was an unheard-of luxury.

"Go down to Johnson's, it's six houses down. They've got fowls. Ask for an egg — an' mind yer don't drop it."

Whew — talk about carrying a piece of expensive china!

Dad boiled it, and took it upstairs along with a plate full of bread and marge, and Dan and I stood by the bed whilst she ate it.

She carefully cut the bread into short strips to dip into the egg. We watched every movement with fascination. And then every other piece of yellow tipped bread went into our mouths in turn.

And today I buy a dozen eggs without a second's thought.

Chapter Three

WITH our Dad being a collier there was never any shortage of coal at our house, apart from the 1926 coal strike. But I'll come to that later.

The miners were allowed a ton of concessionary coal a month. The cost? A shilling for the coal and four shillings for carting. The delivery was done with horse and cart, the coal being tipped up outside the house.

Many a time I've seen Mam get it into the coalhouse when it was delivered after Dad had gone on the afternoon shift. She'd borrow a neighbour's barrow for a penny, and load in the huge black, shiny lumps with Dad's spade. Then, her fat arms wobbling with the exertion, she'd wheel the barrow load down the entry, round the bottom of the outbuildings, and up the red brick yard to the coalhouse. Then she'd start shovelling again.

She told me many years later that even when she was expecting, she used to get the coal in. It's a wonder it didn't kill her. But that was Mam — tough as they come.

Of course there were no washing machines at that time. Only ponches and dollies, and tubs. The tubs were huge wooden things, and must have held gallons and gallons of water. Those who were better off had the smaller zinc tubs and zinc dollies.

Mam always washed on Wednesdays. "Nasty temper day", we kids used to call it. Either the copper fire wouldn't light, or it would start to rain. Sometimes it took ages to boil the copper full of water. Mam would shred "Sunlight" soap into the water, and keep stirring it with a smooth copper stick. No soap powders. Just hard soap and plenty of elbow grease, and the ponch. The ponch was like a heavy milkmaid's stool at the end of a long, thick stick. How it used to thud - thump - thud - thump.

Then the wet clothes would go through the huge wooden rollers of the mangle. Then either into the rinsing water if they were coloureds, or the copper if they were whites or towels.

And all morning and sometimes part of the afternoon, Mam would be shovelling slack on to the copper fire. It was often late in the afternoon before the washing was finished, the huge tub rolled on its side to discharge the last of the water, and the heavy iron mangle pushed back against the wall.

Then, and only then, would we dare to approach Mam.

When it was dinner time she'd nip into the house to cut some slices of bread, and we'd have cold meat or black puddings for dinner. There were no school dinners if you please. Our mothers were responsible for seeing that our bellies were kept well filled. And we were healthy too.

When it was wet on washdays it would be God help us if we got in Mam's way. Smoke would blow down from chimneys on to the wet clothes, or gusts of wind would whip out the pegs, and send the sheets trailing across the wet yard. And then we'd hear the full range of Mam's vocabulary. But this poem I composed in later years will better explain what washday was like:

Snowy white sheets,
Huge sails flapping in the sky.
Baby's nappies, soft as thistle-down.
A row of Dad's socks, unromantic,
Keeping company with the dusters.
A regiment of towels sparkling clear
With a thirty minute boil.

Cotton frocks and pinnies
Bobbing wih gay abandon.
White school socks and hankies,
Striped pyjamas and nighties
Sandwiched between, subdued by
Dad's night-shirt, and Mam's
Voluminous flannelette nightdress;
And, discreetly on a line at the back,
Her unmentionables,
Huge balloons in pink and blue.

A spattering of rain
From ominous black clouds
Bringing down soot and smoke
From a nearby chimney
And ear-splitting words
From Mam's vocabulary.

Baby howling for his feed,
Dad demands:
"How long 'fore dinner's ready?"
In tones that mean:
"I want it now."
Wind increasing in its fury
Scattering socks and pegs
Like falling Autumn leaves.

A sudden crash as a line breaks,
White sails grovel on garden soil,
Kids rush for shelter
From Mam, now swearing
As only a collier's wife can,
"Damn the rain! Damn the smokel
Out of my way,
Damn wet Wednesdays!"

One day when Mam was stoking up the copper fire she found she'd run out of soap.

"Just nip round to Pembleton's shop for a bar of 'Sunlight'," she told me. "Tell her to put it on the slate."

Just as I got to the top of the entry there was a funny noise coming from the sky. All the kids on their way to school were looking into the air, as were their mothers seeing them off, and the few men who were at home. The noisy sort of drone came nearer, and then we saw an aeroplane. There were not many about at that time, at least not our way.

The plane looked huge, and menacing, and I was fascinated. It didn't seem to be going much faster than I could walk, and I hurried so's I could keep up with it, my head held back looking up until it hurt. But by then I was at school.

All the kids were rattling on about it at school. It was the topic for that morning's lesson, and I had made up my mind that I would learn to fly when I grew up. If girls were allowed to do that, of course. But my dreams soon faded when I got back home.

"Where's my bloody soap? Why didn't yer call at th'shop like I told yer to? I've had to fetch it mesen. I've a good mind to give yer a good hiding."

But she didn't, only I wasn't allowed to go out that night to play on th'oller.

But Mam wasn't always tough and swearing. She'd got her soft side. There was a packie (trader) used to call. You could have things on the never-never, the old system. They call it "hire-purchase" today. This man had dealings with several stores, including furniture stores.

In one of the leaflets this man gave Mam was a selection of gramophones, one in particular which she liked. It was a square table model with a lid. "His Master's Voice". So Mam decided she'd have this one. It took her ages to pay it off at a shilling a week.

Now up to this time there was never any music in the house, apart from our singing. No radios or anything like that. Some people were getting wireless sets, the better-off folk, but not us. Mam bought some small seven-inch records from a music shop up town. Her choice amazed me at first. Strauss's "Blue Danube", "Peer Gynt Suite", "Poet and Peasant Overture", and some of Gilbert and Sullivan's music. Not bawdy pub songs, or anything like that.

She would sit there at the side of the table turning the gramophone handle. Then the music would start and a dreamy, wrapt expression would come over her face, and she'd be in another world. The sound would start to slow down, and she'd wind the handle again like fury, back out of her dreamlike state.

Talk about pride of possession.

Our Dad was a singer. He'd got a deep bass voice. He wasn't

in a choir or anything, just used to sing at the pub at weekends. But on Sunday mornings he'd start to sing when he was frying the breakfast. Bacon and tomatoes. Tarantellas. And they were tomatoes, not like some of today's sorry-looking things floating around in coloured water.

Dad would balance the large frypan on top of the fire. First the bacon. But he was usually so engrossed in his singing, the rashers would be too crisp and dark brown. He'd shove it on to a waiting plate which he popped into the oven. Then he'd pour in the luscious tomatoes, a whole large tin. And all the time he'd be going through his repertoire: "Annie Laurie", "The Old Rugged Cross", and one I've never heard anyone else sing, then or now. The words went:

"Gathered by the angels to the land of rest, music sweetly flowing through the sky". He'd really let it rip, till he'd stop to see what Mam was shouting from upstairs.

"Where's me cup o' tea? And don't burn that buggerin' bacon!"

When the tomatoes were cooked enough, Dad woud call upstairs: "All right Nellie your Highness, you can come down now, breakfast is served".

Dad's Sunday morning cooking was a ritual, as was his walk afterwards.

He'd go out on his own for a long stroll, then he'd be back regular as clockwork for a saucerfull of peas, the soaked variety, which Mam would have simmering on the hob. Then off he'd go to the pub were he'd stay for a couple of hours, and back home for his hotted-up dinner. We'd already had ours.

This was when he'd start to argue. When he'd had a belly-full of beer. Mam only had to say one thing out of place and he'd start, picking on any little thing. Poor Dad stuttered badly. I used to feel real sorry for him, and would hold my breath until he'd got his words out; of course, the beer made it worse.

After dinner he'd go straight up to bed, where he'd stay until about six o'clock, have his tea of cold brisket, then off to the pub again, which opened at seven.

I hated Sundays. Hated the arguments, the swearing, and above all I hated the smell of beer, stale beer, and he beer-smelling urine in the po under the bed.

I think, above all, I must have hated the effect the drinking had on my dear, gentle, kindly Dad. And I swore I'd never marry a man who drank as he did, and if he started drinking heavily after we'd married, then I'd leave him.

I must have idolised my Dad so much I wanted him to be a saint. A human failing, like drinking too much, was something I did not want to associate him with.

Many a time when I said my silent prayers in bed I would mutter: "Please God, let Dad stop drinking". I might have added: "Then maybe I can have a sewing machine".

Chapter Four

FRIDAY night was a special night for Dan and me. That was when we got our pocket money, a ha'penny for Friday and a penny to put by for the pictures on Saturday afternoon. We always tried to be especially good on Fridays, making sure we did nothing at all to displease our Mam.

As soon as we were given our money, off we would go to walk the whole length of Cotmanhay Road, where we lived. It was a good mile long, with plenty of shops and beer-offs which sold sweets. We would look in every window to see who offered the best value, the most sweets for our money. Then at the end of our reconnoitre, which usually lasted about an hour, we would make our purchases.

I favoured blackjack toffee, a sort of layered caramel, black and white. It lasted for ages and ages. Or else I'd buy tiger nuts, or a few sticks of locust. The tiger nuts had a flavour all their own. They weren't much to look at — more like dried up bits of wood — but they lasted a long time. The locust was a long, brown shiny pod, with little black seeds inside. To eat it you had to clamp your teeth hard on the pod, then yank it away from your mouth. Just like a collier taking a bite of thick twist before going down the pit.

Our Dan would probably buy bullseyes, or sugar-coated fishes. Then we would pool them and share them out.

Our pals would be spending their Friday night pocket money too, and we'd stand under a gas lamp and talk, or play Ticky or Lurky. Lurky was a game where we'd all hide, except for one, who had to stand facing the lamp post with closed eyes, and count up to fifty. Then he had to find where we'd hidden, and try to get back to the lamp before we did, shouting "Lurky-one-two-three!"

We did a bit of knocking on doors and running away. And Spirit-Rapping was one of our more sophisticated games. We'd select two houses on opposite sides of the street; Then we'd stick a pin in each door, and tie a length of cotton with a button on each end, the button dangling just under the pin. With another piece of cotton from the centre of the long strip we'd hide behind a wall, or in a front garden.

Then we'd start to pull, gently. Tap tap - tap tap. We'd be crouched in our hiding places with bated breath, or with a fit of giggles. And all at once a door would open, or the two simultaneously. We'd almost stop breathing.

"What's up Mrs Brown? Did you hear summat too?"

"I thought I did, Mrs Flint - a sort of tapping."

Then she'd look down at the door.

"It's them perishing kids agen. Wait till I catch yer, yer boggers!"

But by that time we'd be down the entry and over the wall at the bottom of the garden, and in another street.

But we were never deliberately destructive. I can't ever remember breaking down railings or smashing windows. Vandalism was an almost unheard-of word.

Friday night was barrel-organ night. Round about 5.30 we'd hear it playing outside the pawnshop, which was a daft place to stop anyway, because the people going in had no money, and those who came out were not likely to want to give away that which they'd just bargained for, often with their cherished possessions.

But the old organ grinder would be standing there beside his wood and canvas music-maker, belting out the pops of the day, turning furiously at the handle and hopping about from one foot to the other, trying to keep warm.

Then he'd move on and stand outside the pub, where he did a bit better for coppers. We'd follow him for an hour or so, until he disappeared into the "Jolly Colliers" or "The Trumpet", and we'd go home or on to another session of Spirit Rapping, or down on th'oller.

Saturday afternoon, just after one o'clock, we'd set off for the pictures. There were four to choose from, about a mile and half from where we lived, and mostly uphill. But we always walked. There were the trams, but you had to pay to go on those, and we only had our picture penny.

Inside there was the usual deafening noise which you'd expect from several hundred kids. The better-off ones would pay three ha'pence and go on the balcony. And they'd peel their oranges and throw the skins over the balcony edge at the less fortunates below. But the kids below would throw the peel back until there was a right battle raging. And all at once the cinema manager would walk down the centre aisle, and the babble would miraculously cease.

We'd be able to hear the piano then. A lady came along to play every Saturday. She started to play a half hour before the picture began. She would bang out the favourites of that day, "The Red Red Robin", "I'm Forever Blowing Bubbles", and lots I've now forgotten.

She'd play all the way through the picture too, the tempo increasing in sound and vigour as the picture got more exciting, or modulating to softer music when there was a love scene. She'd sit there looking up at the action on the screen to get her cue.. How that lady's neck must have ached!

I loved the romantic pictures, and thrilled to the gentleness of Janet Gaynor, with her pretty little face and the dimple in her chin, and the look of adoration she gave her lover, Charles Farrell.

And all the way home my head would be in the clouds, and I'd be Janet Gaynor, or Lillian Gish, or Jeanette MacDonald, or a straight-faced dramatic like Greta Garbo. My brother Dan would be going on about something or other, but I'd not want to talk. I was in my own little dream world.

I must have been a most impressionable youngster. I suppose I still am — impressionable.

When we got home there'd be black puddings for tea, all steamy hot. Or there'd be chitterlings, or scratchings. I've not seen scratchings for ages. They were bits of pork fat fried to a delicious crispness. I've even seen people take them to eat in the pictures instead of sweets.

And of course there was always home-baked bread. I can't ever remember Mam buying a shop loaf. She used to bake twice a week, a half-stone of flour at a time. She used a big pancheon, red outside and shiny yellow glaze inside. How she would thump and knead that dough!

Which was the subject of another nostalgic little poem in later years:

Huge fire ablaze,
Mother — fat arms akimbo
Watches as yeast bubbles like volcanic lava
In a pit of snowy white.

Such a thumping and pounding follows,
Only equalled by the sound
Of a washday ponch and tub,
Or the cement mixer
On the road outside.

Fascinated I watch
As the creamy dough billows
And rises, up and over
The mixing bowl.

Delicious, barmy, captivating smells
Fill the house — as, one by one
The dough-filled tins disappear
Into the oven.

And I anticipate the following meal
With such a hunger,
That bids the clock go
Just a little faster.

Later — much later — with tummy full
And crumb-strewn table,
I bless the Lord for Mam
And home-baked bread.

After tea on Saturdays Mam would take a tram ride to the market, which was on top of a hill. Our town is built on a hill. The stall holders would be lighting their paraffin flares before it got dark. Nowadays they are all packed up by five o'clock.

When we were kids that was when the fun would start, the bargaining and spieling begin. We kids would stand, fascinated, listening to the yarns the stallholders would be telling, trying to get people to part with their money. The butcher man was marvellous to listen to. He'd be swaying on his feet. Well. . .there were five pubs around the market place, and a fellow had to wet his whistle, I suppose.

"Nar jushe look wha' ar'm givin' away. One nishe newly-married couples' bit, an' on top thish lump o' stewin' meat. Shome chops an' a bit o' skirts. 'Ere y'are — TWO BOB THE LOT!"

Mam would be there on the front row, shouting the odds. When she got home she'd put her large newspaper parcel on the table, and we'd crowd round to see what bargains she'd got. There was always a long piece of brisket with the bone still in. There'd be all sorts of odds and ends, with sometimes a huge marrow-bone or two. The dripping they produced was out of this world.

Mam would often bring pots back, too. Odd cups and saucers, dishes, dinner plates, all for a few coppers. And she'd bargain for them, too. She sounds tough, I agree, but she had her sensitive side.

One night when she got back from the market she was distinctly peeved about something.

"What's up Mam?" I asked.

"That cheeky bogger on th'pot stall — made me look real daft he did."

"Why, Mam, how?"

"Well he'd got some po's in one corner. I asked him — quiet yer know, 'How much is them po's?' "

"And then what Mam?"

"Why — he shouts out loud so's everyone could hear: 'What missus, d'you mean them Jemimas?' I didn't half feel a fool."

There was the linoleum man on the market, too. A big man with a skin like a crocodile, He had two huge, strapping daughters. They'd got faces to match their stalwart bodies, faces the colour of leather from their exposure to the elements, I suppose. The old man would command them:

"Fetch that roll from over there!" and he'd bang away at the top of a wooden crate.

"Tell you what — I don't want two pound, nor even thirty bob. Twenty six — twenty five. 'Ere — I tell you what I'll do — gimme a pound, an' I'll most likely go bloody well bankrupt."

The daughters would stand there on either side of the length of lino, ready to roll it up again, faces as inscrutable as the Sphinx. I used to marvel at their strength, but they seemed to be so much under the old man's domination, it wouldn't have surprised me to see him use a horsewhip on them.

Then there was the toffee man. There were several toffee stalls where you could buy anything from slabs of Radiance and black-jack to bullseyes and peppermints and sugar-coated fishes, all at five pence a pound.

There was a one-armed man used to stand for years on what we called the Little Market. He had a toffee stall, and several small boys helping him. Years later, my husband told me he was one of the boys on that stall. But I never noticed him — I was too intent on the toffees.

But there was one huge van which used to open up to a sort of platform outside. This toffee man, Bargain Joe, had several others helping him; lackeys, as we knew them. He'd get a large bag, pop in a half-pound block of chocolate, then proceed to add other items: a couple of creamy whirls, a slab of Radiance toffee, a tin of peppermints. We would watch fascinated.

" 'Ere — half a crown the lot. No? Well seeing as 'ow yer such a miserable-looking lot o' buggers an' it's startin' to rain - two bob."

But he'd eventually drop the price to one and sixpence, filling up bags with an almost unbelievable speed, bandying with his customers and lackeys as he did so.

" 'Ere Archie, stop pickin' yer nose. Lady over there wi' the feather in 'er 'at. This one's fer Santa Claus over there. Another fer Mrs 'Arrison. 'Ow's the ode man missus? Still tickin'?"

I could only suppose then that her husband was a clock repairer. I didn't understand half the jargon being bandied about.

Oh, it was one of the highlights of the week to be allowed to go up to the Saturday market. There'd be Mam with her newspaper parcel of meat and pots, and, occasionally, though not very often, one of the huge bags of sweets off Bargain Joe.

Often our pockets would be bulging with apples and oranges and nuts which had rolled off the fruit stalls. Of course, some of them would be a bit squashed from rolling under people's feet, but we'd cut the bruised bits off when we got home.

Yes — Saturday was truly a red letter day for Dan and me.

Chapter Five

A THING I greatly missed as a child was not having grandparents to visit. I never knew either my paternal or maternal grandmas. They died long before I was born.

My Mam's father lived in London, a place called Custom House. He had moved there from Kings Lynn when my Mam and three sisters and one brother were born, soon after his wife's death. When he 'acquired' a housekeeper, the sisters moved out — to Nottingham, in fact, where they set up house together.

Mam never saw my grandad alive after that. When I was six or seven years old she had a letter to say that he had died, and the funeral was in a few days' time.

So Mam contacted the other sisters, and they went to London by train. Mam had to take the baby with her; his name was Harold, and he was just a year old.

So that was one grandad I never saw.

But there was another, my Dad's father. His name was David. After my Dad was born, his mother died, so Dad moved in with some relatives called Hollis, a sister of David's. The old man lived on at his cottage in a slum area of the town. When he grew too old to work he lived off what he could cadge from other people; from Dad, among others, and Public Assistance.

When he got short of coal he'd come to our house with a small sack, or else Dad would take him some round.

I don't think Mam cared for the old man, although she never let him go away empty-handed. There was always a loaf of bread, or a piece of apple pie.

But most of his money he boozed away, and, not being too good on his legs, sometimes he couldn't quite make it to the outside lavatory. Consequently there was often a puddle on the chair where he'd sat When I saw it I was filled with revulsion. I was a sensitive child. "Tissiky" my Mam used to call me.

She would get mad with the old man, too, when she saw the puddle he'd left. I never felt I could be affectionate with him, never wanted to it on his knee. Which was perhaps as well.

One day Mam had to go out shopping.

"I'll not be long. You two behave yourselves," she told Dan and me. We were just wondering what forbidden game we could play, when in walked old David.

"Mam' gone shopping," I told him.

"I'll sit down a bit then, might as well rest me ode legs."

We got on with our game, but I made sure I kept out of the old man's way. Besides, I didn't like the smell which came from him. I hoped he wouldn't leave a puddle, I didn't want to mop it up.

He was staring at me a lot, then he said something which made my young blood run cold, my childish instinct urged me to run.

"You've got a nice little bottom, love; come over here a bit."

I was only seven, but I'll never forget the panic which came over me. I backed away from him, towards the parlour door.

"Come on — I'll not hurt you," he urged. But I was in the parlour and sliding the bolt across the door. Dan followed me in, and was wondering what the fuss was about. I yelled through the door:

"I'll tell our Mam when she gets home."

It went quiet after that, and we soon saw him shuffle by the front window on his way home.

Well — Mam really blew her top when I told her what he'd said. She used all the swear words she could think of, and a few we'd never heard before.

"I'll stop his bloody little game; just wait till your Dad gets home."

But she couldn't wait that long. After she'd given us our dinners and fed the baby, she was off, the baby in the push chair, with a thick grey shawl wrapped round him.

Dad got home and Mam was still out.

"Your dinner's on the hob, Dad," I told him.

"Where's your Mam?"

"She had to go out. She's - she's gone to see Grandad."

"What about?"

But I couldn't tell him. I knew there was something traumatic going on, but my mind was too young to take in the full significance of this family crisis.

It seemed ages before Mam got back. Old David, it seemed, had gone straight to his usual pub when he left our house. Mam had been down to his house, but a neighbour had told her he'd most likely be at 'The Castle' and wouldn't come out until closing time. So she'd waited at the top of the street.

"I gave him a right piece of my mind," she told Dad. "The old bugger'll not come round here again. I'll gi'e 'im tryin' to mess around wi' my kids!"

Dad didn't say much, but he seemed awfully quiet for a long time after that. I never did know if he went round to the old man's about that episode. But about a year later old David had to go into hospital, where he died. Dad went to the funeral, he and his brother-in-law. But Mam didn't go. She kept a rigid silence.

Incest was a word I knew nothing about until later years, but when I look back now, I can understand Mam' wrath. She must have felt like murdering the old man, although there had been no real harm done.

But there might have been. My God! When I think back now of the possibilities. . .

Sex was a word which was taboo in my little confined world, and rape too awful to be contemplated. Anyway, there wasn't so much of it then; rape, I mean. And when it did happen it wasn't splashed all over the headlines and on every page, as it is today. It was spoken of in whispers.

I remember one day a neighbour talking quietly to Mam. I caught odd words. "Oh — was it Lizzie's gel then? I allus did say there was summat a bit queer about that lad." The voices grew quieter when they saw me trying to listen. But later on Mam was telling Dad about it.

It seemed a small girl had been molested whilst walking along a quiet alleyway leading to a beer-off. It was dark, and the youth ran off, but not before someone had recognized him, and found the child weeping. That little happening was a seven-day wonder, so it must have been an isolated case. But for years afterwards that girl was looked at with awe, spoken about in whispers among me and my friends at school. Something-had-happened-to-her. . .

About this time something else happened which was enough to put me off men for the rest of my life. My particular friend of the moment, Patsy Henshaw, had called for me one day. She had her baby sister in a pram.

"Can you come for a walk?" she asked. I looked at Mam. I never did anything without first asking her.

"I suppose so," she said. "Take Harold with you."

So she got the pushchair out and wrapped the thick grey shawl around him. "Behave yourself," she told me. That was all. So we walked along, little mums out with our babies. Two innocents.

We turned off the main road, on to a lane which led to some waste ground. That was where we met the old man. He was shuffling along, his shapeless, baggy breeches hanging in folds around his legs. He was wearing a cloth cap and muffler. I remember quite clearly the dewdrops hanging from his nose, the saliva at the corner of his mouth, and the brown shadow which stained his upper lip, that of the compulsive snuff-taker.

"Hello, little girls — and where might you be going?" he said. "My, my, you have a nice couple o' babies there."

We chatted to the old man, about school, the pictures, our pals.

"And do yer often come round here?" he asked us.

I'd never seen this old chap before, so I was a bit wary with my answers. Oh, we'd been warned against speaking to strangers, but this old man — phew! — he was harmless-looking. All the same. . .

"Let's sit down here a bit shall we?" he said, and we two innocents sat one on either side of him on the grass.

There was no one else about. There never was at that time of day. I felt uneasy, and more so a little while later when he took hold of my hand and moved it towards his trouser fronts. It was then when the uncanny instinct of childhood took over, and I pulled my hand away and got to my feet.

"We've got to get back. Our Mam's said we'd to be back by four o'clock. Come on Patsy."

"What a shame you've got to go," the old man said, all sort of sorry. "Shall yer be comin' this way termorrer? 'Ere, I'll gi'e yer a penny each, an' another one if yer come agen termorrer."

Those pennies looked a small fortune to us, so we pocketed them. We didn't know what else to do.

"Shall you come?" Patsy asked me.

"I dunno — it don't seem right somehow," I told her, still with that feeling of guilt.

We knew nothing of the facts of life at that tender age, and although we were becoming vaguely aware of where babies came from, we'd no idea how they got there.

When I got home Mam was busy baking. I wanted to hide the penny somewhere — but not in the house, she'd be sure to find it. So I got an empty matchbox, and while Mam was down at the lav, put the penny in it and hid it in a corner of the outside window sill.

But I'd forgotten Saturday was when Mam cleaned the windows all round. I just froze when she got the window leather out. And a few minutes later:

"What's this doin' here? Elsie, I'm talkin' to YOU. Who put this here?"

"What — what is it Mam?" I tried to bluff. But there was no bluffing our Mam. I'm sure she was psychic.

"All right — where'd you get it from? Who gave it you?"

"It — was only an old man, honest Mam, He — he were all right."

"What did he give you this for? He must've given it you for some reason. WHAT DID HE DO?"

"Honest, Mam, he didn't do anything."

But I felt all sick inside, and after a while the whole story came out.

"Are you sure he didn't do anything else? Christ — I wish I could get me hands on the old bugger. But I'll tell you one thing, me gel, you'll not shift from this house tomorrow."

I started to cry.

"And you can shut that!" I didn't realise then how frightened she must have been. "I'm goin' round to Patsy Henshaw's mother. I suppose he gave her some money as well."

MEN! OLD MEN! As I said before, it was enough to put me off men for the rest of my life.

Chapter Six

AS long back as I can remember we always went to Sunday School. At first we went to a Methodist Chapel, which I didn't like very much. Well, once a year they'd have an anniversary, and I'd have to sit up there on the platform with a lot of other kids, and we had to recite poems. Everybody would be looking up at us, only it seemed they were all staring at me. It made me feel all shy and self-conscious. I'd go sulky and forget my lines.

Dan would stand there like a little soldier, as did the other boys. The girls would be swaying about, pulling out the bottom of their needlework dresses to show how wide they were, or turning their corkscrew curls around their fingers. How I hated it.

But there was one thing I liked about the chapel. It was when we were allowed up at the back of the organ. It was an organ which had to be kept pumped with bellows, to keep the air going around the pipes. Percy Wheatley, his sister Maisie and our Dan and me would be standing around, waiting to pump the bar up and down. The organ sounded horrible if we forgot to pump, which often happened if we started larking around.

Perce and Dan often disappeared into the room behind the organ, leaving us two girls to pump in turn. They'd be sniggering when they came back, and before long they'd be off again.

"Where you been?" we asked. "What d'you keep going in there for?"

But they wouldn't tell us, until one day when the visiting preacher was preparing for the monthly communion service.

"But this bottle is almost empty," the Reverend gentleman told the Church Officers.

"It can't be," they assured him. "It's only used once a month. Oh dear. . ." as they inspected the contents, ' there won't be enough to go round."

"The Lord will provide," the preacher told them as he topped up with water till the quantity was enough for that day's service.

But by then we knew why the boys so often disappeared during organ practice.

"You two had it, didn't you?" I accused Dan and Perce afterwards. And they had to confess. But they didn't take any more.

Shortly after that we moved to another Sunday School. This was at a big, red, tin tabernacle. It belonged to Cotmanhay Church, and boasted of the largest membership of any Sunday school in the town.

Once a year we had a tea party. There would be a band, and it led us all around the streets. There was such a long procession that sometimes we came upon the tail end walking up a street which we'd previously come down. How I loved marching in time to that band! I was filled with an immense feeling of patriotism. And later on our tummies would be filled with the many potted meat sandwiches and slab cake we'd scoffed.

A few pieces of cake and a tart or two would find their way into my pockets, and these I would proudly present to Mam when I got home.

Every so often there'd be a special service, and we'd be expected to take some collection. But Mam could never afford to give us any. One day I was near to tears because I hadn't any money.

"What's up with her?" Frank Wibberley, one of our pals, asked Dan.

"She's got nowt for the collection plate," Dan told him.

"Ere — wait a minute," Frank said, and ran back to his house. When he came back he put a penny into my hand. A whole penny. That brought on more tears, but for ages after that he was my hero. When he knew I liked to read he gave me a book. It was called "What the Moon Saw". I can't remember what happened to it over the years and I've tried to find another copy, but without success. It was full of short stories covering every part of the world; every part where the moon shone, in fact — hence the title.

This book must have been my first initiation into the world of literature.

I was good at writing essays at school — words just came naturally. I suppose I got it from Dad; he liked making up stories, but he kept quiet about it — I don't think he ever told Mam. He must have done his scribbling down at our allotment garden; he never did any at home.

One day he'd got a rather large envelope in his pocket. He told me he was going for a walk. But his walk took him to the "Advertiser" Office. A long time later he told me about it. He'd written this story, "The Victoria Cross", and wanted to see it in print. But when he got to the newspaper office his courage deserted him, and he came back home. Poor Dad. I never did see that story. I think he must have burned it.

This same newspaper ran a Children's Corner. One week there'd be a competition for an essay, and the next for a painting. Dad encouraged me to have a go.

Now drawing and painting was something else which came naturally to me, so I thought I would try. A Day at the Seaside, the competition was about. I'd never been to the seaside then, so my imagination had to work overtime. But I got first prize. A lovely book which I could choose for myself. Uncle Toby, the Editor, shook hands with me, and I felt so proud — as did Dad when I got home.

Next week there was a story competition, so of course I had

to have a go at that, too. My story was called "The Cherry Orchard", and was about a picnic I'd enjoyed with my cousin Gladys from Nottingham. Again I won first prize.

Now, if you won two weeks running you had to get the best results twice more before you were awarded another prize, Handicapped, they called it in the Children's Corner. How I loved that word, and how it spurred me on to greater things!

By the time I had left school I had fifteen prizes to my credit. I still have the books, still treasure them.

And all that began with "What The Moon Saw", which Frank Wibberley gave to me.

There was another boy we used to play with, and whom I had a crush on. His name was Harry Straw. He was tall and thin, and had fair hair. A blond Adonis, I used to think at the time. We all went long walks together, and played all sorts of games, some of them not very nice. One particular one we called Catch The Bird. We would prop up a dustbin lid with a piece of stick, put some bread as bait underneath, and tie a long piece of string to the handle. Then we would hide behind a fence and if a sparrow started pecking the bait — well, I leave you to guess what happened.

One day we saw someting brown disappear under the lid, so we pulled hard at the string. You should have heard the commotion which followed, the squawking, and the feathers flying. Harry's next-door-neighbour ran out to rescue her brown Leghorn which was frantically running around, the dustbin lid still on its back, and its feet entangled in the string.

That was the last time we played that game.

One day we were playing cricket with Harry in their wide entry. Our bat was a piece of wood and our ball half a brick. It was my turn to bat, but cricket has never been my strong point, so I just swiped blindly with the bat. Wham! Crunch! The brick landed on Harry's head, on his right temple. Well, I just dropped everything and fled when I saw blood.

Mam was out, the door locked, and I hid in the lavatory for ages before I dare venture out again. What if he died? Would I be hung? Well, I would be a murderer. I'd go to prison for sure.

I felt all sick inside. But I had to find out what had happened, so stealthily I crept round the outbuildings at the bottom of our entry. I peeped round the corner, and was looking up at the tall figure of Fanny, Harry's eldest sister. I've never, ever forgotten that feeling of fright.

"What yer been doin' to our Harry?" she shouted at me. I could only babble out a few incoherent words.

"I didn't do it on purpose, honest I didn't."

But I felt an immense relief when I knew that he wasn't dead after all. And so cricket was taboo for a long time after that.

Most of the kids' fathers round where we lived worked at the pits. Not all of them: a few worked at the factory, as warpers and knitters. But Dad started down the pit when he was only thirteen years old, and he was almost seventy before he finished work, still a collier. We used to hear of bad falls, and men getting buried, and there was always a terrible fear at the back of my mind that this might happen to Dad.

One evening he went on for the night shift. I'd seen him change into his grey flannel shirt and tough moleskins after he'd had his supper. I'd put his boots by his chair, and watched as he wrapped the toe-rags around his feet. These rags helped to cushion his feet when he was kneeling on the pit bottom.

He never talked much about his job. Just accepted it, I suppose; accepted the fact that he'd be clearing muck away for the rest of his life. He'd be off by nine o'clock, walking the three miles to the colliery in time for the ten o'clock shift.

I'd felt uneasy that night. I must have been developing some of Mam's psychic powers. When I heard Dad's key in the lock next morning I lay, listening. Usually I heard him poke up the raker on the fire, and clear out the dead ashes underneath. Then he'd clomp across the yard to the wash-house to fill the kettle for his breakfast. Mam didn't get up until later.

But that morning there was only silence. After a while I crept downstairs and quietly opened the door. Dad sat here before the dead fire, his head buried in his hands. I couldn't see his face, but the back of is head looked horrible. There was a pad or something held roughly in place with plaster. But the pad was soaked with blood, and more blood had run down his neck, on to his shirt band. It was a ghastly sight.

"Oh Dad — ducks, what have you done?" He turned to me and his face looked white under all the coal dust, if that is possible. He was covered in sweat. It must have been a nightmare for him to have walked home in that state. I hurried round, making him a mug of tea. Somehow he managed to wash himself without passing out, and I got some more got water ready, and clean rags.

How I cleaned that wound without throwing up I'll never know. There were bits of pulpy flesh hanging round the deep cut, and they came away on the cloth I was using. I put some Milton in the hot water and bathed away until the wound looked clean. Then I put more clean rag across and held it in place with sticking plaster. Apart from an occasional drawing in of his breath, Dad never made a sound. And when he was sitting back in his own armchair later, he said: "You're a good lass, our Elsie." I felt sort of choked up inside.

He had to go to the Hospital next day to have stitches in the wound. But for the rest of his life he had a big blue, semi-circular scar on the back of his head.

His way home from work led him through the lovely Shipley Woods, and often he'd tell me of the birds he'd seen, or a rabbit or squirrel, and one day a fox. He'd describe the early morning sun filtering through the branches, thick overhead, and occasionally he'd bring home a young, abandoned bird, or one which had been injured.

He'd got a packet of bird food at home, and he would mix it with warm milk, and with a fountain pen filler would pour drops of the mixture into the bird's beak.

Some of the birds died, and that would be sad. But others recovered, and Dad would wrap them in a bit of soft tissue paper, place them in his large hip pocket, and release the bird when he reached the wood again.

He was so gentle. If he'd been better-off he would probably have been a professor of something or other, or an ornithologist. It was difficult to associate so gentle a person with the hard graft of the coal miner.

Chapter Seven

I VIVIDLY remember one day in early November. Dad gave us a penny each and told us to "get lost" for a couple of hours. We couldn't believe it. Not the "getting lost" bit, but because it was only Wednesday. We never, ever, had pocket money on Wednesdays — only on Friday and Saturday.

"I reckon there's summat up with our Dad," I said to Dan. He agreed. Well, he had to, I was older than him. . .

"What shall we buy with it, an' where shall we go?" Dan asked.

"I know — let's go along the canal as far as Potter's Lock, then we can come back through the cemetry. We can get some tuffees at the terminus end."

The terminus was where the trams turned round, and the long pole was unhooked from the electric wires, to be brought on to the return wire. There were several sweet shops there. That's where we would spend our pennies.

"Better put your boots on," Dad told us, "it's muddy."

"What we got to go out for Dad?" I asked.

"Never you mind," He looked worried. "Cause your Mam's badly, that's what for. She's goin' to lie down for a bit. Now mind you don't get into any trouble."

And so we set off. We spent our pennies at the terminus. I bought some Black Jack. Mmm. . .lovely gooey toffee, and Dan bought locust and monkey nuts. We shared them as we went along, six monkey nuts for one piece of toffee.

All at once Dan started to cry.

"What's up with you?" I asked him.

"D'you — d'you think our Mam's going to die?"

"Course not, dafty. What makes you think that?"

"Well — our Dad says she's badly, an' you do die when you're badly, don't you?"

Gosh! I'd never thought of that.

"Oh — she won't die," I told him with more conviction than I felt. "She's too fat."

"Mr Jones died, an' he was fat," Dan sobbed.

"Silly — he fell off a ladder, didn't he?"

But he'd really started me thinking. What if our Mam did die? She was poorly, and just lately she had been lying down a lot. I'd had to go errands for her, and sweep the yard and clean the lav. I didn't like cleaning the lav, scrubbing that big wooden seat with that horrible pan underneath. But I daren't grumble or I'd have got a clout.

Our Dan had stopped crying by now, and we'd reached the canal. There was a tin can floating on the water, and a dead dog. There were often dead dogs. I used to shudder at the sight. If I'd had a dog I wouldn't ever have drowned it like that. But Mam wouldn't let us have one. Said she'd enough to do feeding two-legged 'uns.

We threw stones at the tin can, but some men higher up the canal shouted at us. They were fishing. They glared at us as we passed them, so we daren't throw any more stones.

We walked along until we reached the cemetery gates. We went along one side and read all the names on the grave-stones, then started to walk between the graves, reading those as well. I tried to visualize all the skeletons lying below us. It was a lovely, eerie feeling. Suddenly Dan started to cry again.

"Now what's up?" I asked him.

"I wonder if they'll bury our Mam here?" he sobbed again.

"Oh shut up, cry baby." But I was frightened, too, by this time. "I know — let's say our prayers, then maybe she'll get better; only you got to mean it," I emphasized.

We had just reached a big stone angel.

"Let's kneel down here," I told Dan. "But you mustn't laugh, and you must close your eyes." So we knelt down there and put our hands together. I peeped at Dan. His face was all wet, his nose had started to run and was mixed up with the tears.

The angel is still there, slightly the worse for wear, but I look at it now with a nostalgia which brings a lump to my throat.

"Please, God, don't let our Mam die," we prayed on that day. And I'm sure the angel smiled at us. Suddenly I had a smashing idea.

"I know — why don't we take our Mam some flowers?" I said. "There's plenty here."

"But that would be stealing," Dan answered.

"Softy! We can take one off each grave. They'd never miss one."

So we quietly nipped around the graves until we had a nice bunch of chrysanths. Then we squeezed through the railings at the bottom of the cemetery so's the keeper wouldn't see us.

When we got back home I looked up at the front window. But the blinds weren't drawn, so Mam must be still alive. I put the flowers in a jar of water in the wash-house. Dad was sitting at the table eating bread and cheese, a mug of tea at his elbow.

"Is our Mam. . .?" I daren't say "Is she still alive?"

"She's all right now," he told us. "You can go up an' see her if you like, 'fore you has yer tea." So we tiptoed upstairs. Mam lay there looking pale. But she was smiling. She looked so pretty with her long brown hair hanging round her shoulders. We were used to seeing it in a bun at the back of her neck. She'd got a flowered nightie on, too; I'd frilled the lace round the neck and cuffs. She looked real pretty. I was so relieved at seeing her alive I let out a big sigh.

"Are you better Mam?" I asked.

"I'm all right now. Where've you been? Has yer Dad told yer? Come here, I've got summat to show yer," she said, and pulled back the bedclothes. I stared. I coudn't believe it.

"But it's a baby Mam. It's ANOTHER BABY! Is it ours? Can we keep it? Shall we have to send it back?"

"I should hope not," Mam said. Our Dan just stood and gaped, his nose still wet. I crept a bit nearer to look. This was a pretty baby, pale pink skin, black hair and long eyelashes. Not like some I'd seen who looked like dried prunes.

"Is it a. . .?" I began.

"Yes, it's a girl," Mam told me.

Then I remembered.

"I got you something Mam." I rushed downstairs, into the wash-house, grabbed the chrysanths from the jar, and flew back upstairs. I couldn't speak, I just held out the flowers.

"For me?" Mam said. "Oh thank you Elsie." Her eyes were wet all of a sudden, and I was a bit choked up, too. "Oh, they're lovely." If they'd have been made of gold she couldn't have been more pleased. I was glad she didn't ask me where I got them from.

Our Dan was still staring at the baby, but he'd picked up one little finger in his grubby hand.

"You ought to wash your hands first our Dan," I told him. "D'you want it to catch germs off'n you?"

"He's all right," Mam said, patting his head. "You must take care of him and Harold 'till I get up again." Then she asked me to fetch her a cup of tea. I'd have fetched her anything she wanted right then. I'd have gone back to the cemetery and gathered her all the other flowers.

I was singing as I went back downstairs: "Mam's got a baby, I've got a sister." Dad laughed at me, and I felt all sort of warm inside as he poured out the tea.

Mam was better, she wasn't going to die after all. Oh, I did love her so much, and my Dad too.

"Please God, thank you for making my Mam better," I prayed into my pillow that night.

Chapter Eight

A FEW weeks after the new baby was born, Mam started to prepare for Christmas. She made all her own mincemeat, Christmas puddings, cake, pickled cabbage and pickled onions. She let us help with the stirring of the puddings and mincemeat, and I loved the smell of the spices and the richness of the fruit and grated apples. I wanted nothing to do with the onions, though. Mam would pickle whole jars of them.

She had a recipe for ginger wine, too. She made pints of it, but I thought it horrid stuff, so biting to the palate. She never bought sherry or port. That came much later when we kids started work.

But we loved our Christmases. We always had one good toy each. At first mine would always be a doll, but later on it was paints and paint books. Our Dan would have a wind-up train set, or something else with wheels on. There were sweets, apples and oranges, and most years a new toothbrush. We didn't use toothpaste; that came much later, too. We used a mixture of soot and salt, but it hurt your gums, and I was glad when Mam could at last afford to buy toothpaste.

There'd be a rabbit for dinner on Christmas Day, and occasionally pork, but not very often. We'd stuff ourselves until all we wanted to do afterwards was laze about, too full to play with our toys.

But on this particular Christmas, when the baby, Marian, was a month old, Aunt Ethel and Uncle Will came over from Nottingham to see Mam. They had Cousin Gladys with them, and they'd walked. It was eight miles away, and there was a thin layer of crisp snow covering the streets. There was the occasional bus, but they preferred to walk. no doubt to save money.

After expressing admiration at the baby, and sampling some of Mam's pies and cake, they prepared to leave for their long journey back home.

"How about letting Elsie come back with us?" they asked. Mam looked surprised. I was a-quiver with excitement.

"D'you mean spend Christmas away from home?" I said.

"You can go if you want to," Mam told me.

So we set off to Nottingham in the crisp starlight, a journey which took about two and a half hours. I'd never walked so far before in one go. But what a Christmas!

Besides the usual mincepies and pudding, there was a rich cake with icing on it, a goose, brazil nuts wrapped in dates, lots of chocolate and cream biscuits, and port wine and sherry. And there was a whole cooked ham.

I used to think Aunt and Uncle must have been very wealthy, but now I realise that with only one child, and Uncle with a good job at a furniture shop, well, they'd more money to spare than us. Besides, Uncle didn't go to the pub same as Dad, spending all his spare money on beer. But how I revelled in the apparent luxury of their home!

We didn't hang our stockings up on Christmas Eve, but Gladys said not to worry — "He'll be here just the same. . ."

Next morning there were two identical boxes outside the bedroom door. I stared, speechless.

"Go on — see what you've got," Gladys told me. There was a red, gold-trimmed box full of chocolates, a hair brush, new ribbons, and a box of hankies, a big thick painting book, a reading book, besides apples and oranges and sweets pushed round the edges to fill up. I felt all choked up inside. I wished Mam could have been there to see it.

It had snowed again during the night, and it looked like a real Dickensian Christmas Card. After breakfast Uncle Will got the sledge out, and we trundled off to the Forest. I'd never tobogganed before, and found it a most exhilarating experience, but when I went down the slopes on my own I invariably sped straight for a large tree, to the amusement of the experts.

But what an appetite it gave us, and how I enjoyed that dinner — and there were real sixpences in the pudding. After dinner Gladys played the piano (yes, they'd got one of those, too!) and we sang carols, and she played "Poet and Peasant Overture" and "In A Monastery Garden". But when she started on "In A Persian Market" I did an impromptu belly dance, with pieces of net swirling from my hips. And when they clapped me and begged me to do it again, I decided I'd be a dancer when I grew up instead of a lady pilot or a film star.

On Boxing Day, Gladys and I queued outside the "Empire" to see the pantomime. We were going up in the "gods", so we had to wait a long time. By the time we'd walked round and round the spiral staircase to the roof I felt dizzy, but I forgot all that later when I watched the splendour and lavishness of "Aladdin and his Wonderful Lamp". I was in another world, a fantastic dream world, and I didn't want to come down to earth again.

We were right in the middle of the front row, so we had to wait ages to file out when it was all over. I just sat, reliving the experience. I put my hand under the seat to retrieve my gloves, and found something else. A purse. A shabby one, but a purse nevertheless.

"Come on," Gladys said. But I was searching through my find. One compartment was filled with loose, strongly-perfumed face powder, but in the other was one shilling and sixpence. A small fortune.

That the purse was someone else's property bothered me not

the least. Finding's keeping, I thought at that time. Besides, now I'd be able to buy a real present for Mam. I put the money in my pocket, and left the purse where I'd found it.

The following afternoon we went to a birthday party across the street from my Aunt's. It was the first party I'd ever been to, the first time I'd played party games.

Lillian Fountain, whose party it was, had a fantastic Aunt. She did a thought-reading act. We all had to write a question on a piece of paper, which we then folded. The Aunty stroked the folded paper across her forehead, pondered deeply, and then answered the question in a mystic voice. And she was right every time. We were all amazed at her powers. And for years afterwards I was puzzled as to how the thought-reading act was done.

Inevitably it was time to say goodbye. The party was over. And next day it was time for me to go home, too. I was seen safely on the bus to Ilkeston, my head still full of the new life I'd been permitted to taste for several days. I felt a desolation creep over me at the thought of leaving it all, at the thought of the near-poverty I was going back to.

But then I felt the one and sixpence in my pocket. There was a Woolworths store opening shortly in our main street. "Nothing over sixpence" the posters on the windows proclaimed. Mam suspected nothing when I asked to be allowed to go up town for the opening.

The store was lofty, with big plate-glass windows. A string quartet was playing behind potted palms, and the place was crowded. The glittering set-out on the counters made it look like an Aladdin's Cave. Then I saw them. A pair of aluminium photo frames, polished to a brightness that made them look like silver. Sixpence each, the ticket said — so I bought the pair. I still had sixpence left. I looked at boxes of handkerchiefs, lisle stockings, scarves, but they were too ordinary. Then I reached the stationery counter. There were writing cases; some looked as if they were covered with leather, some with flowers, but there was a beauty with a country scene with cottages. Inside were pink envelopes and paper. That was it. So with my precious purchases in separate bags I made my way home, the sweet music of the violins still in my ears. I had been in paradise.

And the look on Mam's face when I proudly presented her with the gifts made my young heart glow.

Of course she wanted to know where the money came from.

"I found it, Mam, at the Empire." That seemed to satisfy her. She found a wedding photograph of her and Dad, and another of Dan and me in our anniversary clothes all stiff and self-conscious. She fixed them in the frames, and they adorned our dresser for many a year, taking some of the glory from the "Stags At Bay" on the wall above.

And the notepaper was fetched out once a month, "Cause it's my turn to write to Ethel," Mam would say.

These were the first real gifts I'd been able to give her, but oh — the joy they gave to me!

Chapter Nine

ONE of the things I always found exciting was election times. If it was only the Local Council elections there was so much going on. There would be out-door meetings at the top of Vernon Street — "Vernon 'oller" we called it.

There'd be shouting and wrangling, fists being shaken, swear-words flung about. The women would be there with their grey shawls around their shoulders, many with their husbands' caps on their heads. Mam always wore one of Dad's cloth caps, and she'd metal curling pins sticking out underneath.

She'd be on the front row, shouting the odds as usual.

"What about the workers? When are we goin' ta get a decent 'ouse?"

'Yes — what about it? Eight kids in two fartin' bedrooms is no damn good to us!"

"Bet ee's gorra decent 'aase!"

"Meybe that's why ee comes from t'other end o' town. So's we shanna know too much about 'im. Berr'ee's got enough bed-rooms!" And so it went on.

Housing was a sore point at that time. When hasn't it been? The Conservative candidate would be shouted down. Ilkeston has always been a Labour stronghold. It still is.

Of course the Municipal Elections would produce the usual candidates, often from the working classes, who were trying to get in on the act. The "social climbers" as we knew them. They'd make all sorts of promises about what they'd do if they were elected. And that was about all we got, promises.

We'd see them going off to some function or other, often in their own cars, their wives sitting there like queens, with fur stoles around their necks. You couldn't touch them with a barge pole.

You can't fool the workers for long, and the colliers were a tough lot and not so illiterate as they sometimes appeared to be.

Besides the open air meetings there'd be those in Assembly Rooms, or in Chapel Schoolrooms. They let kids go in, too. That meant that I was always there. I used to lap it all up. The big words the candidates flung about, promising a better environment, a wider outlook on life. For even at that tender age I was thinking for my-self, aware of the poverty and degradation of the lower classes.

I would sit there entranced. I would love to have heckled with the speakers, but my vocabulary was strictly limited. Besides, I was only a collier's kid, I would soon have been shouted down.

But all the way from the meetings the thoughts would be swirling around my head. Why was it that we at our house had to count every single farthing we spent, whilst others around us were living in apparent luxury? Luxury as it appeared to me then.

These were mostly the shopkeepers, or the factory owners. A man who owned a factory not far from us had a house built on a big square plot of land. The house had two windows on the upstairs front, and one on either side of the imposing oak front door. When they took up residence it was as if royalty had moved in. They even had a tennis court at the back. To me this represented the ultimate in wealth.

Today that house looks dowdy and inconspicuous among all the new ones which have sprung up around it.

The election candidates would be promising all sorts of things if they were elected. New houses for the miners, a better standard of living, better schools for the kids. A utopia in fact. But we'd all go on in the same old way: cramped bedrooms; tin baths on the rug in front of the fire; yards and yards of bread and dripping, and suet dumplings; hand-me-down clothes from the better-offs around us. And Mam all the time dreaming of a council house, with a bathroom, and a garden at the back.

Then in 1924 there was a General Election. A new Prime Minister to be brought into Parliament. There were cars going around the streets with red, yellow, or blue ribbons flying from them, loudspeakers blaring away, urging us to Vote Labour — The Conservatives will fight for you — The Liberals will give you a better deal. Then they'd remind you of the meetings taking place that evening.

And of course I'd be on the front row as usual. Dan and I would be waiting for the doors to open. It was a lot better than going to the pictures, and it was all free.

Then there'd be processions of kids marching through the streets, banging their dustbin lids with bits of wood, and singing:

Vote Vote Vote for Mr Oliver
Oliver is the very man
Oliver is the man, and we'll have him if we can,
And we'll knock old Seeley on the floor.

This was a sort of chant. Needless to say, Oliver was the Labour candidate, and Seeley the Conservative.

The colliers and their wives would be cheering us as we passed them, and there'd be more cheers when we arrived at the open-air meeting place.

Mam was always at these meetings, wearing her shawl and her cloth cap. The women would be waving their arms about and singing "The Red Flag" at the tops of their voices. Talk about disorderly conduct! They're a gentle lot today compared with those amazons of 1924.

Naturally, the Labour chap would win. There was never any doubt about that, and when the results were read out later outside the Town Hal!, there'd be a tremendous roar, and more singing of "The Red Flag". Then those men who had any money to spare would go to the pubs and get drunk, and the losers would keep well out of their way.

1924 was indeed a victory for miners. That was when the first Labour Government, headed by Mr Ramsay MacDonald, came into power, and the hopes and ambitions of all the working classes were centred around these leaders.

Would they pull Britain out of the doldrums? Would they make it a country where the working classes would be equal with the more fortunate ones? Time would tell.

But we still had no more money to spend. Mam still had to cut up her old sheets, good sides to the middle, to make new ones, and also pillowcases. We still ate marge all week, although Mam had started to buy a quarter pound of butter a week for tea on Sunday. A quarter of a pound, I ask you! And I was still wearing cast-off black stockings our neighbours, the Wheatleys, gave us.

And there were six of us still living in our two up-two down house in a row. There was Dan and Harold and me in the back bedroom, and Mam and Dad and the baby in the front. There was never, ever, any privacy, and when my figure had begun to develop around twelve years old, it was a work of art to try to undress under the bedclothes.

Our neighbours, the Wheatleys, had a chip shop. They also had four daughters, who wore lovely SILK blouses, beads, and NEW BLACK WOOLLEN STOCKINGS. Every so often Mrs Wheatley, a big women with a merry face and a kind way with her, would give Mam a heap of discarded black stockings — odd ones.

And I would have to pick out all the various shades, various because of repeated washings. There'd be navy-black, red-black, green-black, but never a black-black. I had to pair off all the shades, and wear the blessed things.

But one day, a day I'll never forget, Mrs Wheatley gave Mam a round straw hat one of the girls had finished with. It was our Sunday School Anniversary the following week, and I had hoped that Mam would be able to afford to buy me a new hat. I'd seen one in a shop window. Tuscan straw. Big, floppy brim, lacy, and clusters of pink ribbons around the crown and tying under the chin. But it was only another pipe dream.

"You'll have to make this one do," Mam said, as she proceeded to unpick the ribbon prior to washing of the straw hat I'd had given to me.

You should have seen that hat when it had dried! Crown poking up at the top like an inverted ice-cream cornet, brim drooping all over the place.

"I'm NOT wearing that, our Mam," I told her.

"You'll have to. I can't afford another one. Besides," she added hopefully, "it'll not look so bad if you push the top in," which she proceeded to demonstrate, with the result that it looked more like a dog's drinking bowl.

How I hated that hat! The utter degradation of being on the poverty line, the receiver of cast-offs.

But oh! the joy which followed when Dad said he'd won the football sweep at the "Trumpet". He gave Mam the money to buy me the Tuscan straw hat, and I felt like a princess the following Sunday when I wore it.

The bliss of having something new to wear. Something of my very own.

Chapter Ten

THE following year I was invited to stay at Aunt Ethel's several times. There was a one-man bus service running at that time. It operated from Ilkeston to Nottingham several times a day. Mam would see me safely on the bus Friday evening, and Cousin Gladys would be waiting at the Radford Boulevard crossroads for me.

But oh, the joy of those visits! Besides the excellent cooking of Aunty's, the velvet upholstered chairs and sofa, the floor carpet, the piano playing, there were long walks through the Forest, and the grounds of Wollaton Hall. There were new friends to be made, friends who sounded posh talkers to me, with their unusual accents.

Saturday evenings saw us queueing outside the Albert Hall, where, for one night a week, silent pictures were shown. I loved the loftiness of the great hall, with its palm-adorned raised platform. And I loved the piano playing of the man who sat there all elegant in his black evening suit, tails hanging almost to the floor. He played most of the classics, and a lump would come into my throat as I listened. Music, good music, especially violin playing, always had a profound effect on me. It still has.

When I took the bus home on Sunday after tea-time, I would always feel a little sad.

Then it was Summertime, and an urgent message came from Aunty. They were going to the seaside, to Ingoldmells, and would Mam let me go with them? I'd be company for Gladys.

"Oh Mam! Can I go?" I begged.

"I don't know as how I can afford the train fare," she answered.

But the problem was solved when she learned that Uncle had bought a motor bike and side-car. Gladys was to ride pillion, and Aunt Ethel and I would be in the side-car. A friend of Uncle's was taking the trunk full of bedclothes and other things they'd need. This chap had a van, and was delivering furniture around the Skegness area.

Of course, there was the question of clothes for me, but Mam saw the "packie", and he brought a few dresses to choose from. So Mam bought me two cotton ones.

"Nothing elaborate," Aunty wrote to Mam, "I'll make her some shorts. A few tops will be enough."

The week before we left for the seaside was a pretty tense one for me. I was so excited that I had bouts of diarrhoea and sickness. Mam grated nutmeg in milk and gave it to me to stop the diarrhoea, and gave me soda mints for the sickness.

I was so washed out by the Friday that I thought I'd never be fit to travel. But miraculously I rallied round, and when Uncle Will called for me with the motor cycle combination, I was eagerly looking forward to my first trip to the seaside.

Uncle had hired a converted Nissen-type hut for the week. It was equipped with the usual fold-up beds, primus stove, cheap shelves and cupboards. But it was bliss. It was something different, and when we arrived after our rather bumpy journey, I wanted to go straight up the field to the sea. Up the bank at the top I ran, then stopped, speechless for several seconds.

The tide was full in. The horizon seemed limitless, for I was looking down from a height. I'll never forget the frightening sensation that vast expanse of water gave me.

At last:

"Oh. . .isn't it big?" I managed to gasp out. When I got over my shock at seeing the sea for the first time, I was soon paddling about in the waves. then went back to the hut for the bathing

costume Aunty had provided me with. I must enjoy this new experience to the full.

Gladys and I spent hours just walking along the firm sands, singing, or playing our bazookas, strange-looking tin instruments we bought from "Skeggie". "I'm Happy When I'm Hiking" was the rage at that time, and we gave it full rein.

And the amount of food I managed to put away was astronomical. Besides fruit cake, scones, biscuits, etc., Aunty had boiled a large ham. It was enormous, and the fat layer around the edges was what I loved most. It would make me feel sick now, but it was manna from heaven in those frugal days.

Cousin Gladys was good fun, too. Although she was an only child she wasn't "mardy". She was as tough as a boy, a good swimmer, a real sport.

Ingoldmells was not the caravan city it is now. A few round, corrugated huts, plus a Nissen hut or two, composed the "Haven" site we were on. Billy Butlin's camp came later on, in an adjoining field. There were a few brick bungalows up to Ingoldmells Point — that was all; an almost deserted, shanty-town sort of place. Unspoiled, uncommercialized, but heaven to us.

Inevitably the week came to an end, and it was time to chug back home to Nottingham. But the memory of that week of bliss has never left me. The only disappointment was that Dan could not come with us. But there wasn't room, either in the combination or in the Nissen hut.

Still, Dan was finding friends of his own by then, so I didn't feel quite so guilty.

Chapter Eleven

1926 was a year of traumatic events. By this time I was attending a Higher Grade school. I had passed the eleven plus, but not being fortunate enough to be able to afford the uniform and special equipment needed for the Grammar School, I had to take second best.

Hallcroft School For Girls was a good substitute, however, and all I needed was a navy tunic, blouses, and a satchel. I became a prolific reader, a deep thinker. But I still enjoyed rough games with Dan and the boys.

By the April of 1926 I knew that something momentous was about to happen. There was increased unrest among the coal-miners and their leaders. Mam became anxious, and Dad went about quieter than usual.

It was something about the pit bosses wanting the miners to take a cut in wages. A reduction? They were living on the borderline of poverty as it was.

On April 21st, 1926, a daughter was born to the Duke and Duchess of York. She was christened Elizabeth, and was destined to become our present Queen.

But only a few days after the rejoicing, a coal lock-out and strike was declared. Three days later a General Strike was declared in support of the miners. And in response to the TUC call, transport workers, railwaymen, printers, dockers, and industrial workers throughout the country ceased work. The whole of industry was paralysed, and the Government refused to budge. It was a calamity.

But by May 12th the General Strike was ended, although the Miners' Strike went on, plunging all the coal-mining areas into a morass of discontent — arguing, bickering and abuse being flung from all sides.

The Coal Strike lasted throughout the summer months. Men could be seen hanging about the street corners all day, discontented, not even able to afford a pipe of "baccy", or a pint of beer. The wives grew fractious, finding fault with their men, with the kids, with everything. But upon their shoulders fell the brunt of the outcome of the strike. There was no money to feed the kids, pay the rent, pay the doctor's bills. There was only strike pay, and the money the more careful of the miners had saved over the years.

Mam was never able to save a penny. Dad had always been fond of his weekend pints, his "baccy", and his bet on the horses. But this was looked upon as the miners' privilege, the reward of the hard graft of the week in the bowels of the earth.

Dad's allotment garden was a godsend at this time. Although the potatoes were not yet ready, they were in the ground and getting bigger every day, as were the turnips and cabbages. We wouldn't starve altogether. There was plenty of rhubarb, but stewed rhubarb without sugar took some getting down, and left a roughness on the teeth and an ache in your belly.

Of course the miners' concessionary coal soon ran out, the stocks on the pit tops disappeared, and inevitably searches went on in other places. Farmers opened up their fields, and outcrops sprang up all over the place, on waste ground and even in back gardens.

The men would dig and scrape, often in the foulest conditions. Black damp, the deadly gas, was released from the deepest of the outcrops. Some men succumbed, and had to be treated in hospital. A few died. Some farmers made fortunes selling the bags of outcrop coal to business people.

The outcroppers' kids would be sent home for food and cans of tea; there'd be a regular shuttle service. Some of the mines caved in for want of proper support. In our town even a lorry plunged down in one huge fall of earth.

Our coalhouse soon became empty. Mam had to use lots of coal for baking, and for heating the water.

So — we were without coal.

"Yer'll 'ave ta go coal pickin' same as t'other men," Mam told Dad. Dad didn't much relish the idea, but he set off with a sack and a hand fork; he'd only collected a few cobbles by the time he came home.

"That'll not last more'n an hour," Mam told him. "You two 'ad better go termorrer," she told Dan and me. That suited us just fine, so next morning off we set with the old wooden pushchair and a couple of sacks. We also took some bread and jam, and a bottle of water. We were going to make a day of it.

We traipsed along the colliery sidings, searching for the shiny black diamonds, but so had a lot of other kids and their fathers before us. What we gathered might just keep the fire going for a couple of hours. But this was no good to Mam.

Then, just when we felt like weeping, along came Pete Bradley. He had a smashing barrow, a large wooden box on two pram wheels, and it was full right to the top with bits of coal. He had a big, juicy yellow apple in his fist which he was devouring rapidly — the apple, I mean. He also had more apples bulging from his pockets.

"Hey — where'd yer get that lot from?" We pointed to the coal.

"What'll yer gi'e me if I tell yer?" he mumbled, his mouth full.

"A couple o' marbles," Dan answered. "A conker? It's conkered twenty," he added more hopefully. I was just gaping at the apples. I'd love to have known where he got them from.

So Pete pocketed our prize conker, but in exchange we knew where we could fill our sacks.

Our destination was a desolate piece of waste land which

had been mined many years ago. It was now more like a rabbit warren, riddled with holes where, in the last few weeks, picks had searched for the hidden coal.

There were a dozen or so other kids, with bits of waste metal, old pokers and such like, working away like beavers, their coats slung over the handles of their barrows. They all had their own "bed", and woe betide anybody who tried to trespass on to it!

Gosh, but it was hot that Summer, and this was on exposed ground, being on a hill. We soon found a "bed" of our own, and established our territory by sticking bits of wood in the ground. Being on a hillside it was difficult to find a footing, but we dug our toes in and started to dig. We used the small hand fork of Dad's in turn, and scraped away with our finger nails, too. But we found some grey-looking stuff which we decided was coal, after we'd first pulled the grass and top soil away. After a couple of hours we'd filled one sack, but were now on our knees and our fingers had started to bleed, so we sat down for a while.

And that was when we saw the apples. Huge yellow ones they were, lying on the ground not more than twenty yards from where we sat. But they were in a garden, right under the hillside we were working on, and there was a thick hedge between us.

"Cor! Look at them, our Else," Dan said. "Wish we could get some." By this time we'd eaten our bread and jam, and the water bottle was empty, too. The thought of sinking our teeth into a juicy yellow apple was almost too much to bear, so, while our Dan kept "konk", I slithered down the hillside to search for some means of entry into this Eden. At last I found a hole big enough to crawl through.

I soon had my pockets full of the windfalls. Some were a bit specky, and others not quite ripe. But they were apples, just the same. I hurried back to Dan, casting furtive glances around me as I did so. We sat and munched away until we felt sick, but it was a lovely feeling.

"We'd better take these other apples home to Mam," I said.

"Better not say we pinched 'em," Dan said, "Let's say they'd fallen in th'hedge bottom, and the man in the garden said as we could have them." Our Dan was a clever lad.

Our Mam was that pleased when we got home with two sacks of coal. Well, one and three quarters. The second sack was filled to the top with apples.

"Where'd yer get these from?" Mam wanted to know. So we gave our carefully-rehearsed speech about finding them in the hedge bottom. "I hope yer speakin' the truth. I'd tan yer backsides if I thought yer'd pinched 'em."

But we had lovely apple pie for tea that day.

It was our school holiday, so we were able to go coal-picking again next day. And of course we went to the same place; this time we had Pete Bradley with us. We quickly filled one sack and started on the second. The coal seemed blacker the deeper we dug. I helped Pete a lot. Well, we were all pals together, and anyway I was a bit sweet on him.

"Pete, are we going to get some apples?" I asked. There were still plenty lying in the garden below.

"I tell yer what," Pete said. "Me and your Dan'll go. You keep konk. Whistle if yer see anybody comin'."

So I sat on the hillside and watched them picking up the windfalls. Suddenly, my stomach gave a sickly lurch. I could see a man walking down the avenue between the gardens, and he was making straight for the garden the boys were in.

I whistled, shrill as I could. Dan and Pete came tearing through the hole in the hedge, rushed up the hillside, threw the apples into the sack, and ran off as fast as they could, past the other kids who wondered what all the commotion was about.

I stayed behind and watched from the shelter of a bush. The man couldn't follow through the hole in the hedge — it was too small, and he was a big, powerful man. But he had another gate which we hadn't noticed before. It led on to the waste ground below our hillside.

He fastened the gate behind him and looked round, searching. He saw Dan and Pete, who had by now reached the street leading to the Church. But they were hampered by the pushchair and Pete's barrow. The man ran after them with long, heavy strides. I followed behind at a safe distance, my heart thudding and my knees knocking.

The man was catching up on them fast, and by the time they'd reached the church gates he had a huge hand on their shoulders. He was shaking them, hard.

"Now then — what's yer names, and where'd yer both live?" By this time I had caught up with them and was trembling more than ever.

"Are you one of 'em?" the man asked. I nodded, speechless. We were too scared to give any false names and addresses. The man assured us he would be at our houses later that day, and then he went back to his garden.

We were a sad-looking lot when we arrived home, and our bottoms were soon sore after a tanning from our Mam.

"That'll larn yer to go pinchin'," she said.

We were very sorry for ourselves. We were even sorrier next day, when the big man came to our house with another man, a little bloke wearing glasses.

"This 'ere's the Secretary of the Garden Holders' Association," he told Mam in pompous tones. "There's bin that much stealing from th' gardens just lately, we've decided to prosecute."

"That's right," echoed the little man. "Sorry, but it has to be done. We're calling a meeting tonight."

After they'd gone I felt sick. It would mean prison for us for sure. What would our pals say? And my teacher? I idolised my teacher. Oh! I'd never be able to live it down. I cried and cried until my eyes were puffed up. Our Dan didn't cry. Boys don't, do they? But he was sick before he went to bed that night. He looked horrible.

Mam wouldn't let us go out of the house next day. At tea-time the quiet was shattered by a thumping at the front door. Mam came hurrying from the kitchen, and there at the door stood the big man from the garden, and the Secretary man.

"Yer'd better come in," Mam said, a hard tone in her voice. We stood behind the kitchen door, shaking. "Well — what's to be done about it?" Mam asked. The little man spoke up:

"Well you see — it's like this, Missus," he hesitated. "Fifteen of the garden holders voted for prosecution, and fifteen against. So you see, we've reached a stalemate." He shrugged his shoulders. I wondered what a stalemate was. "Anyway," he went on, "There's Bill Brown as hasn't voted yet. He wasn't at' meetin'. So we've asked him to cast his vote tonight."

"My GOD," said our Mam. "All this palaver for a few lousy apples."

"Sorry, Missus," said the little man, "but rules is rules."

Then they were gone, and Mam was giving us another ticking off.

Next morning, early, the men were at our door again. But this time they had another man with them. He had a plump red face, red and shining like an apple. Ugh! I didn't want to think about apples again as long as I lived. . .

"This 'ere's Bill Brown," said the Secretary man. "Now, Bill Brown has voted against prosecution. So it looks as if the kids'll get another chance."

Then they were gone, but the looks they gave Dan and me made me tremble all over again.

The red-faced man was still there. Mam was thanking him, and shaking his hand. She was so relieved.

"I didn't know they were your two youngsters, Nellie," he was saying. "How's Dan? Does he still like his pint?"

Then he was explaining to Mam why he had voted against prosecution.

"Well — yer see, Nellie, it's like this. I were a bogger fer scrumpin' when I were a kid," he turned to Dan and me. "And they're allus sweeter on th'other side o't'th'edge, aren't they, young uns?"

He and Mam talked for a while — about old times, folks they both knew. I liked this man, he'd got a jolly way with him. I liked him even better when, before he went, he pushed his hand in his pocket and drew out two lovely red apples.

"Here y'are, kids. I shouldn't go pinchin' any more, though. Send them up t'our 'ouse termorrer, Nellie. I'll gi'e yer a bag full."

Chapter Twelve

THE most important issue during the long lean weeks of the Coal Strike was that the kids might go hungry. The grown-ups seemed able to curb their appetites, but the children ran about as usual, and got really "famished".

But the shopkeepers got together, and the publicans, and those who had allotment gardens with root vegetables ready. They pooled meat and vegetables, organised women volunteers and made broth. Several publicans kept pigs, and so had large coppers on their back premises. The broth was made in these coppers, meat, bones, potatoes, carrots and turnips boiled up to make a satisfying whole.

At a set time people would queue up, mainly kids, with their two-pint jugs and large basins. Stale loaves would be cut up into big chunks and handed out with the broth. Then we would go back home, and the broth would be shared among the rest of the family. And our hunger would be assuaged for another day.

One boy we knew, who was a bit simple, turned up one day at the "soup kitchen" with a collander. How we all laughed at the poor unfortunate! But I think of him now with pity.

That the pig swill had been boiled in these same coppers bothered us not in the least. What the eye doesn't see, the heart doesn't grieve. Besides, when you're hungry you will eat almost anything.

It was inevitable that bills were run up at the little grocers' shops, the lists on the "slates" grew longer, and promises were repeated to pay off in full when the miners were back at work again.

I hated going to our shop to buy things "on tick". It was only a small shop, a front parlour really. I don't ever know how the lady at the shop managed to supply so many without payment. But I believe her husband was a factory worker, so they had a regular wage coming in every week. That lady grocer must have had pounds and pounds owing to her by the end of the strike, and I hate to think of the difficulty she must have experienced in getting everybody to pay up. What a terrible time to open up a business.

The "pop shop" (pawnbrokers) did a roaring trade during those long months. Queues would form on Monday mornings, bundles under the people's arms, a hopeless look on their faces — for the outcome of their bartering depended on what the broker thought the goods were worth. Many a heart must have ached to part with treasured possessions — clothes, shoes, and often clocks and watches.

Some colliers and their wives were too proud to be seen going to the "pop shop", and were glad to avail themselves of the local "go between". This lady was enormous, with a huge mop of hair continually hanging in a net, Ena Sharples style.

She did not seem to care how many times she visited the "pop shop", or who she did business with. For make no mistake, she'd really made a business of it. She would collect a few pence for each visit she made, taking the pawn ticket back to her customer. Mam would often say:

"She's off again. Wonder who it's for this time?"

But one day Mam had a bundle of her own wrapped around with brown paper.

"I want you to take this round to Starr's. Ask the man how much he'll let you have on it."

"What is it Mam?" I asked.

"Never you mind," she told me.

"But MAM — I don't want to go there. It's a pawn shop. Only poor people go there."

" An' whatd'you think we are, I'd like to know? Beggars can't be choosers. Now tek this, an' let's have less of yer lip."

So I pocketed my pride and slunk off with the bundle. But I felt terrible standing there in the small, stuffy shop which smelled

of paraffin, stale sweat and urine.

The "go-between" lady was there too, bartering for her customers. She gave me a funny look when I went in, a look which plainly said: "Fancy seeing you here, my fine young lady. I wonder what next."

I pretended I hadn't seen her. At last it was my turn.

"Mam says 'how much will you let her have on this?' " I asked the man. He looked at me over the top of his specs.

"Not seen you here before, have we?" He took the parcel behind a wooden screen. When he came back he handed me a few shillings and a ticket. "Tell your mother this is all I can let her have. It's not a new one."

So I pocketed the money, and wondered what it was that was not new. I gave Mam the money and the ticket.

"Is this all?" she asked.

"Well, Mam, the man said seeing as how it wasn't new, that was all he could let you have."

"God in Heaven, I shall be glad when t'strike's ovver," she said.

"Mam — what was in the parcel? That wasn't new, I mean?"

"Never you mind, nosey," she answered. But for a long, long time after that when Dad had his usual Sunday walk, he wasn't wearing his best suit.

And so the strike went on. Games of football and cricket were organised by the men and youths. Then afterwards they would go down to the canal and swim across the locks, sometimes staying until it was dark. Anything to stop them going crazy.

Women gathered in groups, gossiping, wondering what the hell was going to happen to their families if the strike lasted much longer.

"An' there's Matilda, she's gerrin' on agen. I feel right sorry for 'er," I heard Mam say to one woman.

"She stands need to have any more — 'er's got seven already."

"Well — what d'you expect? Both goin' to bed of a Sunday wid 'News o' th'World'," the other woman answered.

I used to wonder what they meant by "getting on again".

Some of the colliery workers were still slipping off to the pits, maintenance men, I suppose they were. It was supposed to be a total shut-down. If they passed the gossiping women on their way to work, heavens! you should have heard the amazons:

"Get back home, you dirty blacklegs!"

"Strike'll last forever if it's left to you dirty creeps!"

Then they'd start on "The Red Flag" again. The men would leave off their games to shout encouragement to the women.

I wouldn't have been in those blacklegs' shoes for all the coal left in the pits. And these men were shunned for a long time after the strike was over. Even their children were stamped with the dreaded "blacklegs' kids".

I was glad I wasn't one of them.

Chapter Thirteen

AND then suddenly it was all over.

Moleskins were fetched out and shaken, pit boots cleaned. Snap-tins washed and aired to get rid of the musty smell. Water bottles for the pit were washed out with salt. There was the tramp of early morning boots on the pavements once more.

Women sang at their wash-tubs. Bundles were gradually redeemed from the pawnbrokers. Items were slowly erased from the "slates" at the grocers'.

The huge coppers behind the pubs were once more used for their original purpose.

Kids started going to the pictures again, getting their pocket money.

Outcrops were filled in with rubble, and coal carts once more rattled along the streets with their precious cargoes of black diamonds.

You could almost hear the prayers of thanksgiving.

Our neighbours from the chip-shop left to live in another district, leaving some of their furniture stored with us. There was a bookcase full of encyclopaedias and health books. There was one on woman's ailments. Pregnancies.

I spent hours upstairs after that. I would take my homework up in the back bedroom, which I shared with Dan; that was where the bookcase was.

By the time I was due to leave school at fourteen I knew all about babies: how they were formed, what happened to the embryo over the weeks and months, and what happened at the actual birth. How I lapped up that knowledge, because at that time mothers did not think it proper that their children should know too much about sex.

But what intrigued me most was that Mam used to spend hours up there, too. And I thought she would have known it all.

I missed our neighbours, though; they had been such a friendly family, and lots of left-over chips and cold peas had come our way during the strike. But one thing I would not miss was the "hand-me-down" clothes, the many shades of black stockings. . .

I was becoming more aware of clothes, appearances. I was looking forward to the day when I would start work and bring money home into the household.

But I was sad at leaving school. I loved to learn; I respected my teachers; I would sadly miss my school pals. Many of them in the top form had jobs to go to. Several were to help their fathers in businesses; a few to go into offices. Some had shop jobs promised them, and the less ambitious were going into factories.

I didn't want to go into a factory. The factory girls I knew appeared rather coarse and loud-mouthed, with their rude jokes. But shop work, I knew, was poorly paid. I supposed I'd have to take what I could get. Another case of beggars can't be choosers.

I knew what I did want. I wanted to be a nurse. The long weeks of poring over the health books had left me in no doubt about my vocation. So one day, a few weeks before I finished school, I plucked up sufficient courage to ask Mam:

"Can I go into nursing, Mam?" I thought she was going to explode. She couldn't have looked more outraged if I'd have asked asked to become a candidate for the Red Lamp shop.

"NURSING? There's no bloody money in that. Where'd yer get that daft idea from?" She went on and on about it, and I could feel my enthusiasm taking a vast nose-dive, my ego deflate, until I was on the verge of tears.

"What's wrong with a factory job?" she asked me. "Maisie's goin' in th'factory. She's not got silly ideas about bein' a nurse."

"But Mam — somebody's got to do nursing, else what 'ud happen to people when they were ill?"

"Look, our Else," she reasoned with me, "nursing's all right if you've got some other money coming in th'ouse. But there's plenty of jobs at' factory, and it's a sight better pay. Besides," she added more hopefully, "you'll be able to have more pocket money, an' some new clothes." I listened patiently.

Well, I suppose there was some truth in what she said. After all, I was the first of the kids to start work, and I did have some sort of debt to pay off, being clothed and fed all these years.

But at school next day our mistress asked us what we were all going to do. Four were going into shops, had already got the jobs. A few, as I said before, were to help their fathers in business. One girl, daughter of a factory-owner, proudly announced that she didn't have to go out to work at all. Two girls were going on to Art College.

"I could have gone there if we'd had plenty of money," I told my pal. I was still winning prizes from the "Advertiser" for my paintings.

"It's not right," she commiserated. "You're a lot better than they are at painting. It's just not fair." I agreed with her, but it only served to deepen my depression.

I felt worse when it was my turn to tell Miss what I was going to do.

"Mam says I've to go in the factory, Miss."

"FACTORY? Have you girls no ambition? And where do you think the factory will get you? You'll most likely be married to some coal-miner by the time you're twenty, and have several children."

I felt my colour come up at that. After all, Dad was a miner; he was a good man and I respected him.

She poured her sarcasm on the others too, the less ambitious ones who were also going in the factories.

"Really, you might just as well have stayed at the other school." If teachers said half the things nowadays they'd be shouted down.

I felt rebellious after that. Our Dan could see that something was wrong. We still went long walks together, were still close pals.

"What's up, our Else?" he asked me. I had difficulty in keeping back the tears.

"Mam says I've got to go in th'factory, and I know I shall hate it."

"Why don't you run away same as. . .?" He mentioned a boy's name, a boy who had recently absconded.

I thought of me setting out with no money, wandering about to God knows where, maybe sleeping in barns. I thought of my pretty little sister who adored me, and of Harold who was for ever getting into mischief. And I thought of Mam and Dad, and all the years they had fed and clothed me, and the memory of the Tuscan straw hat kept intruding into my troubled mind. I tried to imagine coming home with my first week's wage and giving it to Mam, and the look of pleasure which would come over her face now that she'd have extra money coming in.

I thought of Dad sitting down at his allotment garden, maybe thinking up a few more stories he could scribble down. And I thought of the cosy evenings by our huge fire, with Mam conducting her own private symphony on the gramophone. I thought of Christmases with carol singing, plum pud and mince pies, and the black woollen stockings bulging by the fireplace. I pondered deeply, until my head ached and I felt sick. And at last I answered.

"No — I'll not run away, Dan. I couldn't. I'll just have to go to th'factory after all."

Dan was not a great one for words, but he looked at me so anxiously, and when he fished a couple of caramels out of his pocket and pushed them into my hand I felt like bawling again.

A few days later Mam went to the factory with me. It was a small place with about twenty workers. They did silk winding, and warping and beaming, the end product being a silk jersey fabric.

The factory boss was a prosperous-looking man with a huge stomach and a small, bulbous growth on his upper lip. He asked me a few questions. What school had I been to? Was my eyesight good? Then he said:

"All right, start on Monday after you've left school. Starting pay: five shillings a week."

Mam seemed so pleased that I'd got a job, and she kept looking at me in a funny sort of way. I could sense that she was a bit sorry that I'd had to go into a factory after all, and not been able to do what I'd really wanted.

My last few days at school went rapidly. Essays and paintings were taken off the walls, exercise books put into folders to be brought home, and school reports handed out.

I was top in the form that last term, with "excellent" written beside English Literature and Art. "Elsie is a keen pupil who has worked really hard throughout term" the remarks at the end said. We all said our "goodbyes", and as I waited in the road outside for Dan (he was at the same school, boys' section) I looked back at the building in which I had spent so many profitable years. And the lump was there again in my throat, and the building became blurred.

When I got home Mam gave me that funny look again, then said:

"I'll take you up town termorrer. Buy yer a new frock and some pinafores fer d'factory." I gave her my school report to look at. Mam said, "I'm glad yer've been behavin' yerself."

Dad read it more slowly: "Good marks for English, gel. I'm glad ter see yer taking after me a bit." Then he, too, was looking at me in that same funny kind of way.

"Never mind, Elsie, maybe some day you'll be able to do what you set yer heart on." It was the longest speech I'd heard him say for many a day, and he had a job to get the words out, stutterer that he was.

But my heart warmed towards him, and I'd've loved to have thrown my arms around his neck, but we didn't go in for such great shows of affection. So I just said:

"I'm glad you're pleased Dad."

The next day was Saturday, and with Mam wanting to take me shopping, Dan and I didn't go to the pictures that afternoon. Mam bought me a brown dress — said it wouldn't show the dirt — and two printed pinafores. When we got back home by teatime, Dad said he was going to the pictures.

"D'you want to come with me, Elsie?" he asked. Did I? I most certainly did. Apart from family walks on fine days it was the first time I'd been out anywhere with Dad.

So, after five o'clock we set off on the long walk back into town again. Dad stopped at a shop on the way and bought some monkey nuts. They were really peanuts but we always called them monkey nuts.

I looked up at my tall Dad as we walked along. He was wearing his best fawn raincoat and his trilby was set at a jaunty angle on his head. He had soaped the ends of his moustache and twirled them into spikes. He had a lean face, with deep-set eyes, and that long, hooked nose. He looked so handsome, and I felt a thrill of pride run through me. My Dad. THIS WAS MY DAD.

We were eating our monkey nuts all through the picture, scattering the shells around us. I was not so litter-conscious then. When we stood for "The King" there was an awful crackling as we trampled on the shells, and I felt the colour come up into my face as we shuffled along the row. But there were all sorts of things lying there on the floor: toffee wrappings, hard scratchings, orange peel, apple cores and even crusts of bread. Some people, it seemed, must have taken their suppers in with them.

Dad took his hat off while "The King" was being played. He was always full of respect for the Royal Family.

I hung on to his arm all the way down the hill. I had never held his arm before, and I felt rather self-conscious. As I said before, we are not a family to parade our affections. I can never, ever, remember being kissed by my mother, nor my father come to that. It seems strange, I agree, but that's how it was.

"Kissin's all right fer mushy folks," Mam would say.

But this awareness of Dad as a man was something new to me, something a little frightening. Maybe it was because I was approaching adolescence; adolescence came later in those days.

But I often look back on that walk home with Dad, at my feeling of pride, at the awareness that I, too, would soon be an adult. It was the beginning of many visits to the pictures together. Dan didn't go. He had his own pals now; they went their own way.

But this new affinity with my father was the beginning of a closer relationship. He talked to me as another person, not as a child. Before, I had looked upon him as the provider of our daily bread, the one who earned the money. Mam was just an unpaid servant, or so it had always seemed; we had just accepted the fact that she would do the cooking, the washing, the cleaning — it was her job. Just as I would expect to cook and wash and clean if ever I married.

But we had a great respect for our Mam, even if it was sometimes tinged with fear, for it was she who dealt out the punishment if we had misbehaved. I was a great one for having the last word, and many's the time I felt the sting of a back-hander from her.

"That'll teach yer to answer me back!" she would say, a triumphant tone in her voice.

I must have sorely tried her patience with my obstinacy, and my "But WHY have I got to do it?"

Dad, now, had never once lifted a hand to any of us. Other fathers, colliers, were for ever taking off their leather belts to mete out punishment. Nowadays they'd be had up for child cruelty.

But I have always maintained most firmly, and still do, that corporal punishment is the best deterrent against delinquency. If we did wrong we expected to be punished. But we were careful to avoid that particular wrong-doing again.

That Dad never inflicted corporal punishment was because he was too soft-hearted. But Mam had no such qualms; she was not vicious, but had decided views on how things should be done, and if not, wanted to know the reason why.

If she had lived today, she would most likely have been a prominent member of the Townswomen's Guild, or the Labour Party, or even made her voice heard in the "Bring Back Hanging" controversy.

But to the end of her days she was a collier's wife, tough, hard-working, her man and her kids' well-being the prime target of her life.

She had a strong sense of humour, too — and believe me, she certainly needed it.

Chapter Fourteen

I WAS hoping our new-found affinity would prompt Dad to ask me to accompany him on his Sunday morning walk next day. But he set off as usual at around ten o'clock, telling Mam he would be home for his saucerfull of peas at half past eleven.

So Dan and I went to Sunday School. . .but my mind was elsewhere, and I can't remember a thing that was said that morning. What would the factory be like? Would I get on all right with the women? Would I know what to say to them? But above all, would I be able to do the job?

I was so restless for the whole of that day. Mam said:

"Why don't yer go for a walk?"

"I don't want to, Mam," I told her. "Anyway, our Dan's gone off with Pete Bradley."

"Well then, get yer drawing book out. That'll stop yer from mopsing about."

So I sat by the kitchen window and tried to sketch the outbuildings, but my eyes kept wandering up to the fleecy white clouds, and the larks striving to reach the highest point in their flight and song. And I felt like them; wanted to spread my wings and lift my voice into the sky, to relieve my pent-up feelings.

But the day came to an end and I still had not flown, nor sung. But neither had I wept. Dad went off to the pub just before seven, and I knew he wouldn't be back until well after ten. A quarter of an hour's drinking-up time, ten minutes to walk unsteadily home — maybe longer if he met up with some of his drinking pals and they got into an argument.

Mam would wait up until just half past ten. If he wasn't home by then, she'd be off upstairs to bed, discretion being the better part of valour in avoiding a slanging match with a man with a skinful of beer.

But she'd leave a note beside a soup plate. "Stewing meat in the oven. Don't forget to turn the gas out and lock the door."

I lay awake for a long time that night. I was thinking about the phase of my life which had just come to an end. I was wondering about the new life which lay ahead, and the anxiety turned my stomach into a hard, tight knot, until I felt drained of all emotion.

I heard Dad stumbling around, knocking into chairs, and I thought of him in his more gentle moments when he hadn't been drinking. And the reluctant tears seemed to squeeze upwards through my throat and out of my tightly-closed lids, and I pulled the bedclothes over my head to shut out the sound of the scraping chairs.

Then all at once Mam's voice broke through the tumult of my dreams: "Elsie-e! it's seven o'clock. Time to get ready fer work!"

WORK? WORK!

Then full realisation broke through my fuddled mind, and I leapt out of bed. Dan was still asleep, so I was able to dress out of bed in comfort. I'd have to wash in the outside wash-house, but I could take a ladle of hot water from the boiler; it wasn't so bad on fine mornings, but when it snowed or rained it was purgatory.

Mam was hovering about me like an anxious hen:

"Look at' clock. Yer'll be late. Yer'll 'ave to be quicker than this in a mornin'!"

"Oh MAM! Don't fuss!" I told her between mouthfulls. Then it was time to leave the house.

"Ere — don't ferget yer pinna'," she said, pushing the printed cotton badge of servitude into my hands.

It was still not yet quite light, and there was a nip in the air. Many feet were echoing along the pavements. Singly or in groups people were hurrying along, hands thrust into pockets, breath rasping in bursts of steam on the thin air.

Then the men on bikes, off to the factories and foundries. A tram clanked past, the driver singing at the top of his voice. A woman called to him:

"Yo sound cheerful this mornin' 'Arry."

"What's the good o' being miserable Gertie?" Harry replied; then he was off on another chorus.

A few colliers were turning into their entries, the smell of their twist tobacco pungent on the frosty air. The same smell now never fails to bring back the memory of that first walk to work.

Then I had reached the factory gates. There was no-one about. S'funny, I thought. . .I later learned that the women had started much earlier, there being a glut of orders to be filled.

I walked up the musty-smelling wooden steps to the winding room. There was a terrific din as I opened the door — the whirling of many swifts, a spoked contraption on which the hanks of silk were stretched. A woman spotted me and came forward.

"Put your coat on there," indicating a row of nails. I did so, self-consciously, and slipped the pinafore over my head, smelling the newness of the calico.

There was another smell, too, overpowering, slightly sickly, which I later learned was the oiliness from the synthetic silk threads.

"Have you brought any scissors?" the woman asked. I shook my head. The woman was plump in a pretty sort of way, fair hair wrapped in a neat coil on her neck, a fuzz of hair around her ears.

"She can borrow these, Edie," another woman said, giving me a friendly grin.

"You've got to stay with me today," Edie said. "I'll show you how to tie a flat knot first. Now, this is how we shake the hanks, and put on these things," which she proceeded to do with a dexterity which made me gasp. I should never be able to do that. She saw my expression. "It'll come to you given time enough," and she showed me how to tie a flat knot.

I struggled on all morning, near to tears several times. But in the end I could tie a flat knot, and my shaky efforts at spinning the silk hanks around my extended hands were rewarded with a: "There you are, you see. I told you it'ud come all at once," from Edie.

"She'll mek' a good winder, given time," the other woman said. Her name, I later learned, was Lucretia. I couldn't believe it — what a mouthful — but everybody called her "Leshia".

That was the total of the winding staff for several years, and from these two friendly women I was soon initiated into the mysteries of "courting", copulation and marriage. They laughed at the naïvety of some of my questions but never failed to enlighten me.

They were like kindly aunts to me, a raw fourteen-year-old, not yet menstruating. The foreman was a warper in the next room, a tall thin man, with an enormous adams apple. He was slightly deaf, and cupped a hand around his ear whenever he spoke to me. But he, too, was kind, and oh, how I needed a friendly word just then! They were all good to me.

At last the first day came to an end. At 5.30 the factory siren went. Machines were switched off, making the sudden silence more profound. The noise was still in my ears.

"Are you seeing Albert tonight?" Leshia was saying to Edie. Edie was courting. She laughed.

"I expect he'll want to go for a walk. But I think we'll be safer at' pictures." I wondered why.

I hung my pinafore on the hook my coat had been on, and was all at once conscious of the ache in my arms and shoulders. I was hungry, and my mouth was dry. I'd be glad when I reached home.

I wondered what Mam would have for tea. Would it be dripping, or jam, or toast, or — and the saliva felt wet around my tongue — would there be a bit of boiled ham or an egg?

I hurried on, conscious that now I was one of this vast throng of workers, going home after the day's toil. Home to a fire, a meal, a welcome from a waiting Mam. And I felt the depression of the last few days slip away like an old wet coat.

I was one of THEM. In a few days I, too, would have a wage packet. When I got home Mam would say: "Sit you down and have yer tea." She'd most likely have my felt slippers warming by the fire, same as she did Dad's. I'd say airily to Dan and Harold: "You can do the washing up. I'm tired. I've been to work." And I'd stretch out on the sofa with my library book.

But when I reached our house I could see the coals had been delivered. Dad was on afternoons, so Mam must have got them in. She was swilling down the red brick yard, and sweating so much you could almost see the steam clouding around her body, like that of a carthorse on a cold day. She was wiping a hand across her nose, adding more coal dust to the layer already well plastered on.

A feeling of disappointment welled up inside me. She shouldn't have been doing this on my first day home from work. She should have been in the living room, fussing over the tea-table, giving me the welcome I deserved.

Then I saw the tired droop of her shoulders, the lines of weariness around her mouth, and I felt ashamed, and full of pity for this woman who worked like a navvy, and asked nothing in return. And I felt a new tenderness towards her, an awareness of what her life was really like, an awareness of my own inadequacy as a daughter. She greeted me:

"How did yer go on? D'you think yer'll like it?" Another rub of the back of her hand over her face, adding yet more coal dust, as she surveyed the wet bricks, the slaky lines of black still clinging to the cracks. "I've not had time to set' table Elsie. Will yo see to it? This lot didn't come until half past three. I've been runnin' all over th' place after a buggerin' barrer. Watsons 'ad broke theirs. I'll be in th'ouse soon as I've finished this. I'll be damn ready fer a cup o' tea, annall."

"Mam," I asked, tentatively, "what's for tea?"

"Why — there's a bit o' cold custard left from yesterday if yer want it. An' there's some nice beef dripping."

I thought of tender, succulent ham and boiled new-laid eggs, just soft enough to dip in fingers of bread.

COLD CUSTARD. UGH!

But I ate it all the same. It wasn't too bad with a dollop of jam on it. Besides, I was hungry.

Mam came in after I'd set out the tea things, her fat arms red from washing under the cold water tap. She'd washed her face, too, but the coal dust still clung around her eyes, making them look enormous.

"Here y'are Mam," I passed her the cup of tea I'd just poured. "Shall I make you some toast?" Then, nervously: "Mam — I shall want a pair of scissors for work."

A swift retort was on her lips. She looked at me, bit it back.

"I'll get yer some at' weekend, when yer've 'ad yer pay."

She wiped the jam off the baby's face, told Harold to wipe his snotty nose, and poured herself another cup of tea.

After the meal I said: "I'll wash up, Mam," and didn't even feel indignant when Dan and Harold started on a game of noughts and crosses.

I was a big girl now. Kids' games were not for me. I was one of the workers.

Mam put the baby to bed, hung Dad's clean night-shirt on the fire-guard to air for when he got home, then got out her gramophone and put on the "Blue Danube".

We sat in the firelight, and the flames sent the shadows flickering about the room, softening the lines on Mam's face. I looked at her as she sat with her eyes closed, a hand swaying to the rhythm, in a dream-world again. I sat on the hearth-rug, my arms around my knees and thought over the events of that day.

And I was glad I hadn't run away after all, had not left the sanctuary of my home. For this was where I belonged, with Mam and Dad and the kids. This was my vocation, my haven. And I would make sure that when Mam and Dad told their friends and neighbours: "Our Elsie's a good girl," I would do my utmost to justify their faith in me.